CW01669578

THE MISSING HUSBAND

An enthralling crime mystery full of twists

ROGER SILVERWOOD

Yorkshire Murder Mysteries Book 13

JOFFE BOOKS

Revised edition 2020
Joffe Books, London
www.joffebooks.com

First published in paperback in
Great Britain as *Wild About Harry* 2009
Also published in eBook as *Missing, Presumed . . .* 2018

ISBN: 978-1-78931-389-5

CHAPTER ONE

POLICE STATION, BROMERSLEY, SOUTH YORKSHIRE. 0832 HOURS. TUESDAY 24 JUNE 2008

The phone rang. He reached out for it.

'Angel.'

The man at the other end gave a quick sigh and said: 'This is Alexander J. Manson, manager of The Feathers Hotel. A very strange thing has happened. During the night, four residents were attacked in their beds while they were asleep, and each one has a nasty injury. I don't like things like that happening in my hotel, Inspector. It gives it a bad reputation. So I wondered if you would look into it yourself, personally…quietly. I really can't do with a lot of uniforms stamping around on my new carpets, making my customers uneasy.'

Angel frowned then glanced at the pile of reports and unopened post on his desk in front of him, some of them more than two weeks old. He rubbed a hand over his mouth.

'Mr Manson,' he said, 'are the injuries life threatening?'

'I don't think so. But the four men have been taken by ambulance to the General Hospital. The injuries were to their hands, and there's blood on the bedding. It will cost a tidy penny replacing the stained sheets and duvets, I can tell you.'

Angel blinked. 'Do you mean all four men suffered an injury to their hand?'

'Yes. The right hand.'

Angel shook his head. It was difficult to believe. He rose to his feet. 'Don't touch their rooms. Leave everything exactly as it is. I'll send somebody over straightaway. Did you say they were taken to the General Hospital?'

'Yes. The A & E department.'

A & E, GENERAL HOSPITAL, BROMERSLEY, SOUTH YORKSHIRE. 0900 HOURS. TUESDAY 24 JUNE 2008

'You wanted to see me, Inspector?'

'Are you the doctor who attended to the four men with hand injuries...from The Feathers Hotel?'

'Yes. The patients with the fractured middle fingers. How come the injury is identical across four patients, Inspector?'

'I don't know. I'd like to know that too. What can you tell me?'

'Looks like the injuries were caused by a tool of some sort being applied to the finger and bent powerfully, causing fracture and dislocation of the second joint.'

Angel's nose and mouth muscles tightened briefly as he listened. 'A tool?' he said.

'Could have been a pair of electrician's pliers,' the doctor said. 'Anyway that's what seems to have happened. But why four men and why all the same injury, I am at a loss to understand.'

Angel shook his head. 'I wish I knew. Where are they now?'

'The last one's in that cubicle at the end. He's just back from the plaster room. The other three, I suppose, will be in the waiting area.'

'Is it all right if I see that man now?'

'Yes, of course. I must get on. Excuse me. There's quite a build-up of patients waiting.'

'Right. Yes, Doctor. Thank you.'

The young doctor darted across to the nursing station and was intercepted by two nurses from different directions, both vying for his attention. The department was very busy.

Angel strode down the centre of the ward to the cubicle with the closed curtains at the far end. He found an opening and peered inside. A man in pyjamas, dressing gown and slippers, aged about thirty-five, was sitting on the edge of a bed looking at his plastered right hand.

'I'm Inspector Angel from Bromersley police,' he said as he pushed through the curtain. 'Are you one of the residents from The Feathers who was attacked last night?'

The man looked up. 'Yes.' He waved the plastered hand at him. 'Somebody broke my finger. A man, I suppose.'

'Did you get a good look at him?'

'I was asleep. Didn't see anything.'

'Didn't he waken you, when he attacked you?'

'No. All I remember is that I was asleep, then I suddenly woke up and my hand hurt like hell. When I put my other hand to it I found it was hot and wet, and I realized it was bleeding. I put the light on… There was a bit of blood and the pain…' He shook his head as though he couldn't find words. 'I was a bit hazy. Must have been the loss of blood.'

'You didn't see or hear anything?'

'No. I told you. I was asleep.'

'Everything in the room…normal? The door closed, locked and so on?'

'Yes. I went in the bathroom and rinsed my hand. It cleaned it up but the pain was horrendous. I rang down to reception.'

'What time was that?'

'Ten past four.'

Angel rubbed his chin. The man must have been anaesthetized at the actual moment of the assault; that's why he wasn't aware of it until he woke up.

'What's going on in that hotel?' the man said. 'Three other men have also had their fingers broken in the night.'

'Do you know them?'

'Of course I don't know them. I don't know anybody in this town. I live in Essex. I am field sales manager for a jigsaw puzzle manufacturer. I was calling on customers in Sheffield and Leeds. I was passing through. The Feathers was a convenient place to spend the night. I shan't be staying *there* again.'

Angel pursed his lips. 'Do you feel as if you'd been drugged?'

'No. But I suppose I might have been. That would probably explain why I wasn't aware of anything.'

'If you were, it would be likely to have been administered in food or drink.'

'I had a meal in the restaurant and a few beers afterwards in the bar.'

Angel nodded. There was a definite line of inquiry. He thought a moment and then said: 'Can you think of any reason why anyone would want to...attack you? To get their own back for something. A grudge? Have you any sort of a... feud with anybody?'

The man's eyes flashed; his jaw tightened. 'What sort of a man do you think I am? Of course I haven't got a feud with anybody. I don't even know anybody in this uncivilized part of the world. I am just an ordinary, hard-working, married man with two kids, trying to earn my living. I am not one of your regular drugged up hare-brained hoodlums stealing and conning my way through life. I came to this godforsaken town to spend a night, one night, that's all, and I get assaulted while I am asleep. And you ask me if I have a feud with anybody! It's bloody outrageous.'

Angel frowned. He seemed to have touched a nerve. He didn't apologize; he might have done if he had thought he had anything to apologize for, but he didn't think he had. He asked to see some form of identity, which created more outraged reaction. The man opportunely had a wallet in his dressing-gown pocket, which contained a collection of credit, debit and store cards, club membership cards, RAC and library membership and driving licence, as well as money. He took out the cards en bloc and handed them to Angel.

He quickly shuffled through them, chose the driving licence, and quickly copied the man's name and address on the back of an envelope kept in his inside pocket. He returned the card promptly and told him he would be in touch later.

The man's name was Stanley Selman of 112 Chestnut Avenue, Moston Barkwith, Essex.

Angel pushed out through the curtains, leaving him sitting on the edge of the bed, scowling at his plastered hand and breathing heavily.

DS Ron Gawber was waiting at the open A & E ward door. He waved to attract his attention.

'I came as soon as I got your message, sir. Been talking to the triage nurse. Strange tale, four men with broken fingers?'

Angel looked round. 'Only you, Ron? I left a message for Trevor Crisp, Ed Scrivens and John Weightman to report here.'

'Not seen them, sir.'

His lips tightened back against his teeth. 'I don't want this case going cold. I've just been talking to one of the four. I didn't interview him in depth. That wants doing. His name is Stanley Selman. The others are in the waiting room — that's this way,' he said, pointing along a corridor. They walked as they talked.

'Very strange, sir. Four men with broken fingers.'

Angel nodded. 'Aye. The same finger on the same hand. There must be some link between them,' he said. 'See if you can find out what it is. Speak to them separately. Go through everything. Employment, education and domestic history. When you've got their identities, ring them through to Ahmed. Get him to check them out on the PNC. The hospital manager might let you have a little room where you can interview them. All right?'

'Right, sir.'

'Crisp, Scrivens and Weightman should have been here by now. Anyway, they can't be far behind. You can brief them. These interviews could prove vital. I'm going to The Feathers, see what SOCO have got.'

They reached the waiting room, which was more of a large hall than a room. Two staircases, two lifts, four corridors to the rest of the hospital and a main exit to the car park. There were lots of chairs and tables. Twenty or more people were sitting around small tables. Some were drinking tea.

Three men in night attire, all sporting matching right hands, sat silent, glum-faced and glaring at their cumbersome, newly acquired dressings.

Angel nodded towards them and then went straight ahead to the automatic sliding doors that led out of the hospital to the car park.

Gawber approached them.

PENZANCE TO LEEDS TRAIN. 1035 HOURS. TUESDAY 24 JUNE 2008

The carriage door slid open and the ticket inspector lurched through into the carriage as the train braked jerkily then surged forward again.

'Tickets, please,' he called, grabbing hold of the top of a seat.

The passengers fumbled into their pockets and handbags.

A man pulled out a brown envelope with 'Probation Service' printed on the top left-hand corner and a copy of the May 2008 issue of *Lady and Home* magazine before he found the HMP rail travel warrant for a single journey from Dartmoor to Bromersley.

The ticket inspector checked the warrant with neither a word nor a glance, then handed it back to the man, who shoved it back in his pocket with the brown envelope.

He reopened the *Lady and Home* magazine to the page with the small ads and read once more the one he had ringed in blue ballpoint.

'Genteel lady living in quiet country house in South Yorkshire, seeks gardener/handyman. Able to drive an advantage. Own cottage. References essential. Apply Box No 212.'

He rubbed his chin thoughtfully.

THE FEATHERS HOTEL, BROMERSLEY. 1042 HOURS. TUESDAY 24 JUNE 2008

As Angel went through the automatic doors of the town's premier four-star hotel, he noticed a skinny man in a smart striped suit handing cash over to the desk clerk at the reception desk. The skinny man then nodded at the clerk, took the bill, folded it, put it in his pocket, picked up a small suitcase at his feet, turned, saw Angel, immediately looked away and made for the automatic doors.

Angel frowned. He thought he had recognized him.

The man dashed through the doors and out to the car park.

'Can I help you?' the clerk said to Angel from behind the desk.

Angel turned to face him. His mind was still on the skinny man in the smart suit, but he said, 'I'm Inspector Angel from Bromersley police. There is a unit of men examining the rooms where some of your residents were attacked last night. Can you direct me to them?'

Before the clerk could answer, a voice from the office behind the reception desk boomed out, 'Upstairs, Inspector. First and second floor. They seem to have taken over the entire hotel.' It was Alexander J. Manson, manager. He appeared in the office doorway and walked up to the desk. 'I should take the lift, Inspector. It's right behind you.'

Angel looked into the man's glaring, inhospitable eyes, nodded and said, 'Thank you, Mr Manson.'

He turned, pressed the button to call the lift, then he returned to the reception desk. He looked at the clerk and said, 'The man you were attending to when I came in… what's his name?'

'Which man, sir?' the clerk said, casting a sly look at Manson, who was still in position.

'The man in the smart suit. Slim. About fifty years of age. I think he had just paid his bill.'

The clerk frowned and consulted a book on his desk.

Manson said: 'It was a Mr Corbett, Inspector.'

Angel's eyes flashed. 'Thank you,' he said and turned away.

His mind started whizzing round. So it was Lloyd Corbett from Manchester. Lloyd Corbett and his brother, James were running the rackets in that part of Lancashire. Whenever there was any major crime in and around that city, the Corbetts were at the bottom of it. Yet the police were never able to prove anything against them. The Corbetts had the lower echelons of criminals over there so scared that nobody would ever give evidence against them. What was Lloyd doing in Bromersley? Wherever he went could only spell trouble. He could have been the attacker of these four men, although he didn't usually do his own dirty work.

'From Plymouth, I think you will find,' Manson said, raising his nose towards the crystal chandelier and pointing to the clerk.

'Flat 11, Nelson Buildings, Forthwith Road, Plymouth,' the clerk read out.

Angel smiled. 'I hope he paid you cash.'

Manson glared at the clerk, who nodded.

Manson smiled.

'Stayed the one night, did he?' Angel said.

'Yes, sir,' the clerk said. 'Room 101. And he had breakfast in bed.'

Angel wrinkled his nose. 'Thank you.'

The lift arrived. The doors rattled open.

Angel stepped into it and pressed the button for the first floor. As it arrived and the doors opened, he saw a sign with an arrow indicating that room 101 was to the left. He went up to the bedroom door and knocked on it. There was no reply. He looked around. The landing and corridors were deserted. He leaned forward and downwards to get an eye-level look at the door lock. It looked easy. He reached into his inside pocket, took out an out-of-date Barclaycard, slipped it between door and jamb, tapped it with the heel of his hand. The latch was back and he was inside. He quickly closed the door. He looked round. He spotted the tray of dirty breakfast pots on the unmade bed. The room had not yet been cleaned. He was in luck. His face brightened. He tiptoed across the carpet to the white telephone on the bedside table. Then, taking the white curly cable loosely, he lifted the phone, dangled it near to his ear and tapped the redial button. He listened. There were some electronic noises then a man's voice said: 'Yeah?'

'This is the telephone engineer,' Angel said. 'I have a caller from Bromersley trying to reach you. There seems to be a fault on your line. Would you confirm your number?'

'Go away, little man,' the voice said. It was followed by an ear-numbing click.

Angel's eyebrows shot up. He yanked the phone away from his ear. That was almost certainly James Corbett. If he had found out the number, he could have obtained the address from the phone company and that would have been the first step in the process of arresting him and his brother, and putting them away. He breathed out a foot of air, and put the phone silently back in its cradle.

There was a knock at the door.

'Hello, yes?' he called.

'Oh. It's all right, sir,' a woman's voice called through the locked door. 'It's only room service. I'll come back.'

'It's all right. Please come in.'

There was a rattle of keys and the door opened.

Angel flashed his warrant card and said, 'I am a police officer. Would you please leave this room exactly as it is until our Scenes Of Crime Officers have checked it?'

Her eyes narrowed. 'I suppose so. But there are four other rooms I can't do. At this rate, I'm never going to finish.'

'Sony about this, but you will have heard that four men were attacked in the night.'

'Huh! Heard nothing else all morning. Not safe in our beds anymore. The police are a waste of space. Disgusting.'

'These five rooms... Did you come across any of the men from these rooms at all, or answer any call from them for room service?'

'Naw. They're too mean to pay the extra.'

He nodded. 'Thank you.'

She turned away to leave.

'Where are the police officers working at the moment?' Angel asked.

She looked back, pointed to the ceiling and said, 'Up one, in rooms 201, 212 and 215.'

'Ta.'

He found the stairs and was soon on the second floor. It was very quiet. There was no sign of life along the landing and the corridors. He found room number 201 and peered round the open door.

Angel immediately noticed an unusual smell.

A team of four SOCOs in white overalls were hard at it. One man was dusting for prints on knobs and handles, edges and ledges where intruding criminal fingers may have wandered, another was transferring the contents of the waste-paper baskets into evidence bags, a third was running a lightweight vacuum cleaner sucking hairs, fluff, threads and human dust over the carpet, curtains and duvet, and the fourth was photographing the room in general, certain vital places and anything out of the ordinary.

One of the SOCOs turned to see him in the doorway. It was DS Donald Taylor. He was in charge of the SOCO at Bromersley. He pulled down his mask.

Angel said: 'What's that smell?'

Taylor looked upwards and sniffed several times. 'Can't smell anything, sir.'

Angel grunted. Then sniffed again. He could still smell it. He thought it must be the smell of new carpet or polish or perfume or disinfectant or something. He wasn't satisfied.

'Found anything useful?'

'No, sir.'

'You'll check for any print of the other three in each of the rooms, won't you?'

'Yes, sir. Of course.'

'Have you found anything at all that indicates a similarity?'

He shrugged slightly. 'Two of them are salesmen.'

Angel blinked. 'What do they sell?'

'One sells tiles, sir. Building tiles to builders. And the other, jigsaw puzzles to…stationers, I suppose.'

He wrinkled his nose. There wasn't much similarity there. 'Anything else?'

'Two of them use the same toothpaste.'

He shook his head. 'No. Anything else?'

'No. There's nothing else.'

'There must be something. Keep looking. Have you done all four rooms?'

'Yes, sir. This is the last. We'll only be five minutes.'

'Right, then I want you to check out their cars. They'll be on the car park. You can get the index numbers from reception. I want you to check for prints of any of the other three in each car, but chiefly examine the tread. See if there is any similarity in the soil content. Let's find out if they've been in the same part of the world, just in case they've been forgetful.'

Taylor smiled. 'Right, sir.'

He turned away, then Angel remembered something else.

'Oh, Don. I also want you to do a sweep of Room 101. It's for a different reason from those four. It was occupied last night by a Lloyd Corbett. He's wanted for all sorts of unsavoury activities. Be sure to pick up his prints, if there are any, to make a positive check with records.'

'Isn't he the brother of James Corbett from Manchester way? I've heard of them. Nasty people. What are they doing over here?'

Angel had wondered the same thing. 'That's him. A lead to where he's been or where he was going could prove invaluable. So…do your best.'

Taylor nodded in a positive, business-like way.

Angel was assured that he would.

'I'll just take a look round the other rooms,' Angel said. 'Have you got the keys or do I have to use plastic?'

Taylor smiled and gave him the hotel keys to 212, 215 and 111. He sauntered into room 212 and again immediately met that unusual smell. He frowned as he looked around. The room was set out like the other two had been. A valise was on the case stand at the end of the bed. He opened it and fished about inside. There was a clean shirt in there, nothing else. He looked into the bathroom. He lifted the cover off the lavatory cistern. Of course there was nothing there. If there had been, SOCO would have found it, but old habits die hard. There was nothing in the room of interest. He looked round room 215 and then went down a flight of stairs, to 111. He could find nothing useful to the investigation in either room. There was nothing to link the four men, unless you counted the same insidious smell. He could find nothing else.

He came out of room number 111, the last of the four rooms, which was opposite room number 101, and bumped into the chambermaid pulling a trolley of clean towels.

'Excuse me,' he began.

She stopped. 'Now what's wrong?' she said.

He smiled to try to warm up the relationship. The response was a cold glare.

'Could you tell me, have any of the bedrooms recently been decorated?' he asked.

'No. Why? What's the matter with them?'

'It's a question of the…ambience,' he eventually managed to say.

'Oh,' she said, her eyes like two eggs in a frying pan. 'And what's the matter with it? I done that room thorough. Bathroom an' all.'

'It's really very…charming,' he said, 'but there is a difference.' He opened the door of room 111 behind him and said, 'Would you allow me to…explain?'

She eyed him strangely.

'Please come inside.'

She hesitated and then slowly crossed in front of him and went into the room. He closed the door.

'What is it? I've got six rooms to do yet. I'm way behind.'

'The smell. Do you not notice the unusual smell? Is it some polish that you use?'

She lifted up her nose, wrinkled it slightly, sniffed several times and said, 'The window needs opening, that's all it is.' She charged across the room towards it.

'Just a moment,' Angel said.

She stopped, turned and looked back at him.

'Can you not smell something unusual?' he said. 'A distinctive smell?'

She nodded. 'It's boiled sweets.'

He frowned. 'Boiled sweets?' he said. He shook his head. 'I can smell this in 201, 212, 215 and here, where the four men were attacked, but I *can't* smell it in 101. Why do you think that is?'

'Because the chap in 101 was probably a chocolate man.'

'Ah,' Angel began. 'Mr Manson, I wonder if you could assist me?'

Manson came up to the hotel reception desk. 'I will certainly try, Inspector. All my staff are instructed to assist you in every way with any inquiries you may wish to make to solve this dreadful business,' he said with a smile that might have turned milk into cheese.

Angel wrinkled his nose. 'The four injured residents must have been heavily sedated if not entirely unconscious to enable such a vicious assault to take place. I need to know if anyone saw a person — say, for instance, Mr Corbett — drop a hypnotic drug into their food or drink during the course of the evening?'

Manson frowned as he considered the question. After a few moments he said: 'I will see. Please wait here. It won't take a moment.'

He shot off and was away only three minutes.

'I have spoken to the staff on duty at the time,' he said on his return, 'and the consensus of opinion is that Mr Corbett of room 101 could not have administered anything to anybody. It is believed that he stayed in his room all evening, as he was not seen in the bar or the restaurant after around 5 p.m. A restaurant chitty shows that he ordered a light meal from room service at 7.10 p.m. The staff seem to remember him, his appearance being…unusual. On the other hand, while they accept that it would easily be possible to drop a foreign substance into a glass of red wine or a beer, they cannot say with any certainty anything about the drinking patterns of any of the four residents who were attacked in the early hours. The staff regret not being able to assist with this information, mainly due to the fact that none of them can recall what any of the four actually looked like. They just seem to be anonymous men in lounge suits to them. The chitties show that while all four dined separately in the restaurant that evening, one of the residents, the man in room 201, Mr Selman, had no drinks at all on his bill. Also, whilst replying to this question, all the restaurant and bar staff hasten to say that they did not see, nor would they condone, the adding of any kind of foreign substance to a resident's food or drink. And I must say, I am entirely in accord with the latter remark.'

Angel rubbed his chin. Things were not getting any better. It was beginning to look as if Corbett couldn't have sedated the four men. Was it possible he had had an accomplice? An inside man, a member of the hotel staff?

'Have you taken on any new staff lately?' Angel said.

'There have been no changes in any department in the hotel here for more than twelve months now, Inspector,' he said, raising his head. 'While good staff are hard to find, so is a good employer.'

Angel sighed. He was blocked at every turn.

'Now, Inspector, is there anything else?' Manson said.

Angel detected an unmistakable impatience in his voice.

'Yes,' Angel said. He would not be put off. 'I wonder if you can tell me when and by what method Lloyd Corbett booked a room here.'

'Possibly, possibly,' he said, and he pulled out a ledger from a shelf under the reception desk top and riffled through the pages. 'You know, Inspector, in a year, hundreds of residents come and go through those doors. We try to make them as comfortable as possible. Every room is let almost every night of the year, so we must be doing *something* right, don't you think? Now, let me see.'

He stopped at a page, looked at it closely and then said, 'He phoned late on Sunday and booked a single room for the next night, the Monday. It was a cancellation. He must have been very fortunate; we are normally fully booked at least a week in advance.'

'Do you have the phone number from where he called?'

'No, Inspector. I do not.'

'What time did he check in on Monday?'

Manson glared at Angel over his thick black-rimmed spectacles.

'We don't have *that* information either, Inspector,' he said as he closed the ledger and slammed it noisily back into its place on the shelf.

Angel stifled a smile and simply nodded.

Manson turned to the desk clerk with raised eyebrows.

The young man shook his head, then said, 'Now I remember, it must have been before three o'clock, sir, because he was in the cocktail bar at the end table. With the door open I could see him from here. A skinny, bald-headed, mean-looking man. Always had a drink in front of him. Kept looking in this direction.'

Angel's eyes shone.

'Ah, yes,' he said, looking at the young man. 'That's him, but how can you be certain it was before three o'clock?'

Manson butted in and said: 'Because he must have bought a drink in that bar before it closed at three o'clock prompt.'

CHAPTER TWO

WARD 29. BROMERSLEY GENERAL HOSPITAL. 1800 HOURS. TUESDAY 24 JUNE 2008

'I'm Detective Inspector Michael Angel,' he said. 'I'm looking for Nurse Frazer.'

'That's me. Thank you for coming so promptly. I am afraid Sir Max Monro is not…very well,' she said, looking at him meaningfully. 'He's eighty-nine, you know. He wants his son, but we were unable to find him. He's very agitated. His BP is very high. He wanted you to bring a recording machine.'

'I have it in my pocket.'

'Good. He asked for that particularly. I'm hopeful that when he has seen you, he will settle down. Will you follow me?'

It was a typical single ward. One of everything. There was an LCD screen at the side of the bed displaying illuminated changing shapes like a range of mountains, and numbers flickering and altering every second or so.

The patient was a white-faced old man with blank, watery eyes. He held tightly on to the edge of the bedclothes, looking first at the nurse and then at Angel.

'Now then, Sir Max. I've got Inspector Angel to see you,' she said, glancing from the old man up to the monitor. She didn't like what she saw.

'I want my son, Nigel,' the old man said in a rich, masterful voice.

'We can't find him, Sir Max. I did tell you. He is not at home. I have phoned several times. I have spoken to your housekeeper. She'll tell him you're in here when he calls. He'll turn up any time, I'm sure. I'll try again in a minute. Don't worry about it.' She turned to Angel and said, 'I'll leave you to it, Inspector. Please don't let him get excited.'

Angel nodded.

She went out and closed the door.

'It's important that I speak to my son,' the old man said.

'Nurse said they were unable to raise him, Sir Max.'

The old man frowned and tried to hoist himself up on one elbow. 'Do I know you?' he said, peering at him with one eye partly closed.

Angel blinked. He understood that the old man had actually asked for him by name.

Sir Max couldn't quite reach a sitting-up position. He sighed and lowered himself back down on to the pillow.

Angel looked down at him and smiled reassuringly. 'I believe you sent for me. We've met a couple of times. I came up to your house two years ago after a burglary. Don't you remember? You had a cat that jumped on my stomach — it was called Noel, I think. Unexpected. Caused me to spill tea on your carpet.'

Sir Max's eyes suddenly opened wide. He smiled. 'It was called Christmas, and I remember it well. You are Michael Angel. You said you had two cats. Still got them?'

'What a memory. Yes. That's right.'

'Oh yes. I remember you. You are a dead straight chap. That's what I need. And something of a whizz at catching criminals, I do believe. Ah yes. That's why I sent for you.'

Angel shrugged. He was embarrassed when people made complimentary remarks. He reckoned he could handle anything but compliments.

'You want to make a statement of some sort?'

'Yes. While my mind is clear. While I can remember the details. I wanted to tell my son, Nigel, but nobody can contact him. He's been looking after my affairs since I had my first stroke three years ago. I have signed everything over to him. I don't know where the hell he is. It's been four days since I last saw him.'

'How can I find him?'

'He's in property, you know. Buys rundown property, smartens it up and then sells it on, or divides it into flats or viable units for offices or commercial uses and leases them out. You know the sort of thing. He's extended into Spain. He's all over the place. He's worth millions. He won't know I'm in here.'

Angel said: 'The nurse said I should bring a tape recorder.'

'Ah yes. That's right. Good. I want to get down the facts. I so easily forget things these days.'

Angel took a recorder out of his pocket, switched it on and put it on the pillow beside him.

'It's very small. Are you sure it's all right?'

'It's what we use in the force every day, Sir Max.'

'Is it recording now?'

Angel nodded. 'Yes. Just speak in your normal voice.'

He cleared his throat and began. He spoke as if he were addressing a battalion. 'This is Sir Max Monro of 38 Creesforth Road, Bromersley. During the Second World War, I was a second lieutenant in the Third Yorkshire Lancers. My regiment was decimated in the early North African campaign, so in October 1944, I was promoted to captain in the field by Major General Sir Hubert Whitty and despatched with a squad of four men to be the personal bodyguard of the Grand Dumas, who was the leader of a sect in the state of Alka Dora in North Africa. The Grand Dumas had made his HQ in a range of desert sand hills on the coast of the Mediterranean. He was a supporter of the Allies and under his leadership his sixty followers had been sabotaging installations in Libya and Algeria, and stealing supplies of ammunition, food, water and petrol, so he was much valued by the Allied Forces. He and his men lived in tents and roamed the desert and so, therefore, did we. We were frequently subjected to mortar-shelling attacks, also subjected to small bombs and machine gunning from low-flying German planes, which meant that we were always on the move. I remember one night we moved camp three times and didn't bother putting up our tents. We simply camouflaged our vehicles and for safety slept under cover of the hot sand 200 yards away from them. Those were horrible nights…and days.

'Anyway, after a particularly hard and difficult night, and two of his best men having been killed in a wave of machine-gun fire, the Grand Dumas said that he wanted to speak to me, where we would not be overheard. We walked several hundred yards out towards the desert. When he was satisfied we could not be overheard, he said that he had a treasure more valuable than the moon. He was deadly serious. He was very solemn, which was unusual. He tended to treat the war as a game; he was usually in high spirits with a devil-may-care attitude. The death of two of his best men earlier that night had clearly affected him. Anyway, in the dark, he took something out of a sort of pocket that was sewn into his cummerbund. It was a wonderful stone, a huge ruby. He let me hold it a moment. It had many facets, and was about as big as a duck's egg. Even at night, in the desert, under the clear star-laden night sky, I could see that it was truly magnificent. It glowed deep red even when the only light was the moon and the stars. He then told me that he had a daughter, Princess Yasmin, who was living in England under the covert protection of the British government, in the Convent of St Peter in the village of Lower Bennington in Yorkshire. He said that the ruby was her inheritance. It would buy her a dowry worth over a thousand camels and it would ensure that she could be honourably married to someone worthy of her. Then he asked me… He made me promise that if anything were to happen to him, that I would take the ruby to her and tell her how much he loved her. Of course, I promised that I would.

'Inevitably, only a few nights later, we were strafed by a German Stuka. The Grand Dumas was killed, my sergeant was killed, I stopped one in my shoulder and some shrapnel in my leg. Our Morris 15 cwt was put out of action. The Grand Dumas's private tent was burned down. Our ammunition truck received a direct hit. It was an absolute shambles. I don't remember how many other casualties there were. Anyway, I crawled over to the Grand Dumas, took the ruby out of his cummerbund and stuffed it into one of my ammunition pouches before his followers took his body away for a very long ceremonial burial.

'That was in March 1945. I was flown next day by helicopter to a field hospital in Gibraltar. Eight days later I was put on a boat at Cherbourg. The boat journey from Cherbourg to Dover was very uncomfortable…up and down those blasted steps into the hold. Thence by a very slow train to Bromersley to St Miriam's Cottage Hospital.'

Angel nodded. He remembered the hospital in his teens. It had since been pulled down in 1980.

Sir Max continued.

'All the while the ruby was wrapped in my handkerchief and stuffed in my left ammunition pouch. Anyway, thank God, I recovered, and could walk tolerably well with a stick. As soon as I could drive, I went up to North Yorkshire to the convent in the village of Lower Bennington to find the Grand Dumas's daughter, the Princess Yasmin, to deliver the ruby. I saw the Mother Superior, Mother Mary Margaret. She was very cagey. At first she was reluctant to acknowledge that she had ever heard of Yasmin, then I managed to draw it out of her that the princess was no longer there, that she had no idea where she was, and that the matter was in the hands of the Ministry of War. I went up to London to Whitehall and spoke to the secretary, who denied any knowledge even of her existence. I wrote to the Minister and explained that I had something valuable to give to her from her father. I got a letter from some clerk to say that the Minister had no knowledge of a Princess Yasmin Dumas, nor any existence of anybody known as the Grand Dumas, and that I was clearly under some misapprehension. I wrote again stressing that the item was extremely valuable and that it was not mine to keep. After a month I got a reply repeating all they had said in the earlier letter and saying that if I wished to divest myself of anything, I could post it to the Alka Dora embassy for the ambassador to dispose of at his discretion. I wasn't prepared to do that. Clearly, HM Government didn't want to admit any knowledge of the Grand Dumas or the Princess. They wanted the matter closed and were not willing to reopen it.'

Angel nodded and said: 'Where is the ruby now?'

'I have it in my safe at home. It has been there all this time. It's OK. It's safe enough. My housekeeper Mrs Dunleavy is living in while I am in here. But it bothers me that I have not been able to settle the matter. I have been unable to find the Grand Dumas's daughter. I am not prepared to hand it over to anyone other than the Princess Yasmin herself. Now, I wanted Nigel to deal with this. I can't imagine where he has got to. Now look here, Michael, this is damned important. That ruby is worth a fortune. It mustn't fall into the wrong hands. If anything happens to me, will you deal with it? Take possession of it and see that it gets to its rightful owner?'

'Well, I'll do what I can, Sir Max.'

'You can do no more, dear boy,' he said as he turned on his side and pulled up the bedclothes. 'The key to the safe is on the bunch among my things in the drawer. The safe's behind the picture of the Queen in my study. Mrs Dunleavy will show you.'

Angel was thinking that if Sir Max hadn't been able to find the Princess Yasmin in sixty years, what chance had he got?

'The Princess might be dead,' Angel said.

But the old man's eyes were closed.

It was ten o'clock the following morning when, with a heavy heart, he pulled up outside number 38 Creesforth Road, Bromersley. He opened the wrought-iron gate, walked up the path, up the stone steps to the big black door and rang the bell. It was soon opened by an elderly lady, who was dabbing her eye with a screwed-up handkerchief. 'You must be Inspector Angel.'

He nodded. 'Mrs Dunleavy?'

'Please come in, Inspector. It's so sad.'

'Yes indeed,' he said. 'I am so sorry. But it was very peaceful, the doctor said.'

She closed the door.

'I thought you were with him at the time?'

'It happened shortly after I left,' he said.

'Please come through.'

'Thank you. Did you know him long?'

'Most of my life. My mother knew Mrs Monro and was housekeeper here for many years. I helped her at busy times and sort of drifted into the job. They were lovely people.'

'You will have grown quite attached to him. Have you heard from his son yet?'

'Nigel?' she said with a disapproving grunt. 'Not a word. That lad has been quite thoughtless these past three years. I don't know what he has been thinking about. The younger generation…'

Angel smiled wryly. According to his calculation, Nigel Monro must have been about sixty years old.

'Now, you wanted to get to the safe?' she said. 'It's in the study. It's this way.'

'Sir Max said it was behind a picture of the Queen.'

'That's right.' She stood at the study door and indicated to him to pass her to go in the room. 'I'll leave you to it.'

'No. No,' Angel said. 'I need you as a witness, if you don't mind. I am here to take one thing only. That's all I will take.'

She frowned. 'Very well.'

He unhooked the picture of the Queen, found the cylindrical-shaped safe built into the wall, with the small door fitting flush with the wall. He peered at the lock, took Sir Max's keys out of his pocket, picked through the bunch for the appropriate one, inserted it and opened the safe. The aperture was only large enough to reach in with one hand. It was mostly stuffed with white envelopes. He took some of them out and put them on the desk. There were four small leather-covered cases containing medals and ribbons. At the back was a torn brown paper parcel. His pulse increased a few beats as he reached in, took it out and put it on the desk. He hurriedly reopened the wrapping to discover a four-inch cube-shaped red cardboard box inside.

Mrs Dunleavy leaned over the desk for a better view.

Angel opened the hinged box lid. Inside was a piece of white plastic sponge moulded to half the egg shape. He quickly lifted it out. But there was no egg underneath. All he could see was another piece of sponge at the bottom of the box; the two pieces together made a mould for the safe packing of the stone.

Angel sighed.

He couldn't hide his surprise and disappointment.

Mrs Dunleavy said, 'Whatever were you looking for?'

He didn't reply.

He turned back to the safe and reached inside to the extreme end of it and withdrew his hand, clutching more envelopes. Then he peered inside. It was empty. All he could see was the polished steel lining. There was positively no ruby egg in there.

Angel said: 'Is there any other place in the house where Sir Max might have hidden anything valuable, Mrs Dunleavy? Another safe, for instance?'

'No,' she said. 'I can't think of anywhere. Sir Max was very…tidy and particular. He used to say there's a place for everything and everything should be in its place. I've heard him say that often.'

Angel nodded.

'Ah well,' she added with a sigh.

Angel began stuffing the white envelopes back into the safe.

'What exactly are you looking for?' she said.

'A ruby egg.'

'A ruby egg?' she said, scratching her head. 'Now there's a novelty.'

'Have you ever seen it?'

'No. And it's not something you come across every day, is it? I mean, a ruby egg? A hen's egg…a chocolate egg…a duck egg even, but not a ruby egg.'

He had repacked the safe with the envelopes and Sir Max's medals and was looking at the packaging that had clearly at one time contained the ruby.

'Was it valuable?' she asked.

'Very,' he said as he found an old label on the package. It was addressed to Sir Max Monro at that address, and it was from 'P. N. Fischer, Diamonds and Gems, 566 Pelikaanstraat, Antwerp'. The post-date mark was April 2004.

'Come in,' Angel called and looked up from his desk.

It was DS Taylor from SOCO. He was carrying a stone-coloured paper file. 'I've got the report on that business at The Feathers, sir.'

Angel's eyebrows shot up. 'Good. Sit down,' he said, pointing to the chair near the desk.

'You'll be pleased to know that we picked up lots of prints in room 101 and the private bathroom, sir, and can confirm that the occupant was indeed, as you had thought, Lloyd Sexton Corbett.'

Angel nodded. He was delighted. It pleased him that he still had the ability to identify a crook he hadn't seen in real life from the memory of a police photograph. It was a pity he hadn't been able to do it instantly; he would have then been able to arrest him.

'Anything to show where he'd been or where he was going?'

'I'm afraid not, sir.'

Angel pursed his lips. He knew he'd need a lot of luck to get an informative sliver of dried mud from off Lloyd Corbett's shoes or a torn-up addressed envelope dropped into a wastepaper basket.

'I'm glad you called in,' Angel said. He rubbed the lobe of his ear between finger and thumb. 'Did any of your team happen to mention the unusual smell in each of the rooms where the four men had been attacked?'

'No, sir. You still think that's important?'

'It's an unexplained detail, Don. It might be important. And it's something that applied to all four rooms, and conspicuously not to the other room which Lloyd Corbett had occupied. It's another unknown factor and I'm stuck for an explanation. I need to find out why four men were attacked and had a finger — the same finger on the same hand — deliberately broken. So what can you tell me? Is there any info in there?' he asked, pointing to the stone-coloured file.

Taylor rubbed his chin. 'Well, not from the examination and swabbing of the rooms, sir.'

Angel frowned. 'Their DNA. Any biological link? Were they related...even distantly?'

'No, sir.'

'What about their clothing? Was there anything similar about their clothes, their personal things or their luggage? Anything the same that might link them?'

'Not as far as we could see, sir. I looked at each man's personal possessions, washing tackle and suitcase, and found nothing that was the same, or even close. There are full lists in the report.'

'Did you think there was anything significant about the location...the arrangement...of the four rooms in relation to the attacks?'

'What do you mean, sir?'

‘I’m fishing, Don. I’m clutching at straws. I’m looking for…for inspiration, for…for ideas. The rooms were not next door to each other, were they? So there was no question that the intruder had assaulted a man in error. They weren’t *all* at the end of corridors. They weren’t *all* on an outside wall. Dammit, they weren’t *all* on the same floor; there was one on the first floor and three on the second.’

Taylor shook his head. ‘Sorry, sir. I really haven’t a clue.’

Angel wasn’t pleased. But his blood was up. His eyes glowed like a cat’s eyes on a frosty night. ‘Are you absolutely positive that there is nothing at all in that report that links those four men?’

‘Yes, sir.’

Angel grunted then said: ‘There *has* to be something more than…than a smell.’ He sighed and rubbed his chin. ‘All right. Thank you. I’ll sort it.’

Taylor nodded and went out.

CHAPTER THREE

There was a knock at the door.

'Come in,' Angel called.

It was Gawber. He had a yellow file under his arm.

Angel raised his head. 'Ah, Ron. Just the man,' he said and pointed to a chair.

'Thank you, sir,' Gawber said. 'I would have been sooner, sir, but I got caught in reception by an angry schoolteacher, a Miss Grimond, headmistress of Striker's Lane School, reporting twenty-eight computers, a reel of black electric cable and a pair of aluminium workmen's steps stolen from her school. The computers had only been installed a week.'

Angel pursed his lips. 'These school robberies are getting out of hand. And it's all public money. And they're so professional. Instruct SOCO to take a look at it. If there is any forensic or anything at all to go on, I'll take a look at it too.'

'Right, sir,' Gawber said and opened the yellow file.

'Did you find a relationship of any sort between the four men?' asked Angel.

'No, sir.'

Angel sighed. 'You've run them through the PNC?'

'Yes, and they're all clean as a whistle.'

'Are they all in proper, full-time employment?'

'One is self-employed. The others are Hugh Adams, aged twenty-nine, who lives in Swansea, works for the Swansea Tile Company and calls on builders. He was in Room 212. Then there was David Baker, aged twenty-five, who lives in London, works for Cheapo chain stores as a field manager of POS printing and ticketing. He was in Room 215. And lastly, Stanley Selman, aged fifty, who lives in Essex, works for Ace Games, makers of jigsaw puzzles and calls on stationers. He was in room 201.'

'Contact their employers and get confirmation that they were in Bromersley, staying at The Feathers, with their full knowledge and approval.'

'Right, sir.'

'Now who is the self-employed one?'

'He is Cyril Carter, aged fifty-nine, who lives in London. He's an antique dealer. Has a shop. Visits auction houses on their viewing days. If he sees anything he's interested in, he leaves bids with the auctioneer, or attends the auction later, or bids by phone live during the auction. He was in room 111.'

'Hmm. That gives him plenty of opportunity to get around without anybody knowing where he is, doesn't it?'

Gawber nodded. 'But I think he is quite legitimate, sir.'

'Probably. But all the same, check on it. Where's his shop?'

'London, sir. SW1.'

Angel wrinkled his nose. 'I want to know how long he's been in business at that address, and at least three auction houses he has bought from in the past few months. Let's see if he is for real or whether the shop is just a front.'

'Right, sir.'

'Did you get anything from the cars? Any similarities there?'

'No, sir. All different makes. No cross prints at all, and there was nothing distinctive in the tread of the tyres.'

So there were the four victims. There was nothing prepossessing about any of them. They seemed like a random collection of ordinary men, just the kind of assortment that might have been thrown together if they had been conscripted for national service.

He licked his lips thoughtfully. 'Did you get the feeling that anyone knew any of the others?'

'No, sir. I would say that they definitely did *not* know each other. There was a certain easy camaraderie between them that had developed because they were all in the same boat, but I didn't observe that they had any history together or knew anything at all about each other.'

'And nobody showed any signs of having a guilty conscience about anything or even hinted why he might have been attacked?'

'No, sir.'

'And you have absolutely no reason to think that any of them were remotely concerned in anything illegal?'

'No, sir. They all seemed highly respectable.'

Angel's lips tightened against his teeth.

There was the mystery. Why had four apparently ordinary disparate honest men had the middle finger of their right hand deliberately broken?

This question would be at the forefront of Angel's mind until he found the answer. He would go to sleep and it would be his last thought, and he would waken up and it would be the first thing to fly into his mind. That's how it was with Michael Angel. He resolved to find the answer, even if it took twenty years. He sighed and ran his hand through his hair.

ROOM 72, TOWN HALL, BROMERSLEY, SOUTH YORKSHIRE, 1405 HOURS. SATURDAY 9 AUGUST 2008

At the end of a long corridor was a sign hung on a door, which read TEMPORARY REGISTRY OFFICE. It was a room the size of a broom cupboard with a table, four chairs and a vase of chrysanthemums.

A small man in a dark suit, white shirt and black tie stood behind the table holding a printed card. He looked into the eyes of the couple standing facing him, and asked each in turn to confirm formally their full name and address.

The man replied boldly, the woman in a small voice.

The small man nodded, cleared his throat and then said: 'Is there any just cause, reason or impediment why you should not be joined together in holy matrimony?'

He leaned forward and looked expectantly from one serious face to the other.

The couple glanced at each other briefly then turned back to face him and in unison said, 'No.'

He nodded, took them rapidly through the vows and concluded with: 'I therefore pronounce you man and wife.'

He sat down, took out his handkerchief and blew his nose.

The only other person in the room, a severe woman in her fifties sitting at the table, pushed a document at the couple. She offered the man a pen and said: 'Sign here, please.'

He smiled at her. She glared back at him.

The young woman standing next to him squeezed his arm, her eyes glowing with passion. She turned and kissed him on the cheek. The man seemingly becoming aware of his tardiness, turned to face her square on; he pulled her towards him, wrapped her tightly in his arms and gave her a fulsome kiss on the lips. Then they sighed and looked into each other's eyes.

The woman tapped her finger on the table. 'Sign here, please,' she said urgently, shaking the pen in his direction.

Eventually the man released the young lady, took the pen, signed the document and passed the pen on to her.

The older woman pointed to a place on the document. The young woman signed with a trembling hand.

The little man from the other side of the table said, 'I hope you will both be very happy.'

His mouth smiled but his eyes did not.

FIVE TREES, LARCHFIELD HILL, SURREY, 0945 HOURS. MONDAY 18 AUGUST 2008

The phone rang. And it kept ringing.

The young woman in the overall glared at it, groaned and said: 'Oh dear.'

She stopped dusting the marble bust of Sir Gregory Line and called out, 'Mrs Henderson! Mrs Henderson! Telephone!' She rushed out of the hall, across the sitting room and through the French windows on to the patio. She glanced round the swimming pool and the garden beyond. There was nobody in sight.

'Are you there?' she called. 'Mrs Henderson! Telephone!'

There was no reply.

The insistent 'brrr brrr' continued.

'Oh,' she said and rushed back inside, past the painting of Sir Gregory Line, which dominated the oak-panelled hall, and up to the phone. She looked at the instrument a brief moment, wiped her hand on her overall then snatched it up.

'Hello. Yes?' she said, her eyes rolling from one side to the other, then back again.

'Oh. Hello, Mrs Critchley, is my sister there?'

The woman's face brightened and she lowered her shoulders. 'No. Oh, it's Miss Selina, isn't it?' she said excitedly. 'It's lovely to hear from you. I can't find her anywhere.'

'Oh dear. Look here, Mrs Critchley. I must speak to her most urgently.'

The woman's eyes suddenly grew bigger. 'I forgot, Miss Selina, you've got married, haven't you?' she said with a snigger. 'Congratulations are in order.'

'Oh dear, I'll have to go,' she snapped, and the line went dead.

The smile left her. 'Hello? Hello?' she said then wrinkled her nose and replaced the phone. She thought Miss Selina very rude cutting her off like that. She had only congratulated her on her getting married. There was nothing wrong with that, surely? Stuck-up cow. Just because they were rich. She pursed her lips and tried to remember where she had left her duster. She looked up and unexpectedly saw the striking figure of her employer standing in the sitting-room doorway. It made her take in a sharp breath. Her mouth stayed open.

Mrs Henderson stared at her. She wasn't pleased. 'Was that the phone?' she said.

'I tried to find you, Mrs Henderson. Honest. I called out. Went out on to the patio. It rang for ages.'

The woman's eyes stared piercingly at her. '*You* answered it?'

'It was Miss Selina.'

Mrs Henderson's face went white. She stepped forward a pace. A hand went to her mouth. Her heart pounded like a drum. She gasped for breath. 'Oh,' she said quickly. 'What did she want? Is she all right? Where was she speaking from? How was she? Is she ringing back? Oh dear. Oh dear.'

*

'Come in,' Angel called.

It was PC Ahmed Ahaz. He was carrying an envelope.

'Just heard back from Plymouth Constabulary, sir. They say there's no such address as Flat 11, Nelson Buildings, Forthwith Road, Plymouth.'

'Thank you. No surprise there, then.'

'Also, this has just come in, sir,' he said, handing him the envelope. 'Special delivery. Looks urgent.'

'Ta, lad,' he said as he slipped a paperknife into the flap.

Ahmed went out and closed the door.

Angel opened the envelope, took out the letter and read it. It said:

Dear Inspector Angel,

Thank you for your letter of 26th June, and I am very sorry to hear of the death of Sir Max Monro. He seemed to be an entirely honourable gentleman.

Regarding the ruby, I was not aware of the existence of such an important gemstone until he sent it to me in March 2004. He wanted me to value the stone for insurance purposes. When I examined it, I realized that this was not a stone that could be valued merely on a carat weight basis. It is of such clarity and of such a weight that it is on a par with gemstones in the British and Russian crown jewels. I therefore advised Sir Max of this in a letter and returned the stone on April 20th 2004 and made no charge for my services.

I hope this information proves helpful.

Yours sincerely,

P. N. Fischer

Angel put the letter down.

He leaned back in the chair. He was grateful to P. N. Fischer for one thing. He had confirmed that the stone was genuinely of great value. It was now obvious that Nigel Monro had upped and off with it. With his money and the ruby, he could just about be anywhere in the world. Angel was wondering how he might try to find Monro and recover the ruby when the phone rang. He reached out for it.

'Angel,' he said.

There was a hoarse intake of breath, which he recognized as Detective Superintendent Harker.

'Come up here,' he said and then banged down the receiver. Angel wrinkled his nose. He replaced the receiver and sighed.

He did not enjoy the interviews he had to endure from time to time with Harker, but he was his boss and he was expected to accept disciplinary direction from his superior in the same way that he doled it out to the ranks below him.

He trudged up the green-painted corridor to Harker's office and tapped on the door. He didn't wait. He took a deep breath and pushed it open.

'You wanted me, sir?'

'There you are, lad,' Harker said. 'Sit down.'

Angel stared at him. The man he was looking at behind that big desk was ugly. Of course, he had always been ugly. He must have been born bald and skinny. Angel looked at him strangely, though, at that moment, as if he hadn't seen him before. The truth was that he saw him almost every working day, sometimes ten times a day. But today was different. The head he could see sticking up through the ill-fitting check shirt with the limp collar looked just like a skull with ears and a chin.

'Well, sit down. What I have to say is extremely important.'

Angel observed him. Harker stuck a white plastic inhaler up a nostril, sniffled noisily, pulled it out, pushed it in the holder and put it in his pocket. He sniffled again then expanded his face in a sort of a smirk — he never smiled — to signify satisfaction with the operation.

'Sit down, Angel,' the skull said. 'What are you gawping at? Are you all right?'

'Yes, sir.'

Harker reached out for a pink sheet of A4 from a wire basket on the desk in front of him. He peered down at it. He read it then reread it, looked up at Angel and said, 'I've a confidential email from the Met. It's for senior police officers only. Privileged information. But you might as well know about it. There's a man wreaking havoc among villains throughout the UK. The Met don't name him because they don't know it. He is referred to as The Fixer. Have you heard your villains or your snouts speak of him?'

'No, sir.'

'Well, they might. The Fixer is said to look so ordinary, so average, so respectable, that nobody has a clue who he is. Yet he is thought to have murdered at least eight men. The Met have heard something of his plans via a judge from judges' chambers. That's why it's confidential. The info is that he is up our way now. That's why they are giving us notice. In return for which they expect us to reciprocate with any information, however slight, of any sort about him.'

'How did he murder these men, sir?'

'Walther PPK/S 32 automatic. He's a crack shot. Never misses. Watch out for him.'

Angel thought about it. He frowned. Hadn't he just said that nobody knew what he looked like? How could he *watch out* for him?

Harker put the email down, placed his arms on the desk and said, 'Now then. This next matter is very serious. I've been checking our postal franking machine bill for last month and it's enormous. It's getting quite out of hand. I've been checking down some of the recent entries and among many various amazing charges, I found a charge for an airmail to Antwerp. The civilian in the post room tells me it's down to you. Who the hell are you writing to in Antwerp?'

'That's in connection with that missing ruby, sir. Sir Max Monro—'

'Sir Max Monro?' he said ponderously. 'He's dead, and he was a very old man. I don't suppose there ever *was* a ruby. Figment of his imagination. There's no crime, is there? Who was robbed?'

'Well, the ruby has disappeared and the rightful owner —'

'Oh yes. A foreign woman.'

Angel's eyes flashed. His mouth dropped open and the muscles round his jaw and throat tightened like a bear-trap. 'A *princess,'* he snapped. 'A *royal* princess.'

'Who *says* she's a royal princess? Anyway, we're not running a lost property office, Angel. I think you're losing sight of the real purpose of your job. Crime and murder is your business. Drop this lost property inquiry. From now on, I want you to utilize your time solving murder cases, and getting villains like the Corbetts behind bars.'

'But while the man was dying, sir — I didn't realize it then — Sir Max asked me to take possession of the ruby, and —'

'But the ruby wasn't there, was it?'

'No, sir. It wasn't. He asked me to —'

'Well, you can't proceed if you can't find the ruby, can you?'

'But I made a sort of promise. Not a promise, as such, but a commitment to see that the stone went to the right person and that's what I intend to do.'

'You gave him *your* word?'

'Yes, sir.'

'That's all right. So it's a personal thing?'

'Yes, sir.'

'Very commendable, I'm sure. But you didn't give him my word, lad, nor the chief's word, nor the force's word, nor the taxpayer's word. Whatever private arrangement you made with the dead man is up to you. But it has nothing to do with your work here.'

Angel's jaw tightened. He felt his stomach thrashing round like a washing machine with a difficult load. Unusually, he couldn't think of anything useful to say.

'And as the man is dead,' Harker said, 'and there isn't actually a ruby and there isn't actually a princess to give it to, your undertaking seems to me to be totally null and void, wouldn't you say?'

The washing machine thrashed more wildly and his pulse began to bang out in his ears. He still couldn't think of a sensible thing to say. He didn't agree but he couldn't immediately counter the apparent logic of what Harker had said.

'So leave that. You can leave these trivial cases in permanent abeyance. Anyway, what usually happens is that — given sufficient time — they tend to come to a natural conclusion. Well, now let's get back to this case of the assault at The Feathers. What is the common link between the four victims?'

Angel's mind was still on Sir Max and the ruby. 'I can't find one, sir,' he said automatically.

'Can't find one? All the modern technology and forensic available to you and you can't find one?'

'Can't find one, sir.'

'You must be looking in the wrong…place.'

'Yes,' Angel said, because it was the easiest thing to say.

Harker's eyebrows shot up. He was amazed at his answer. 'Oh? Well, stick with it. Persistency pays. We all know that. Keep at it. That's all for now, lad. Better get back to it.'

Angel came out of the office, closed the door and stormed down the green corridor, his mind in turmoil. He was met by Ahmed. 'There's a phone call for you, sir, from Wakefield FSU.'

Angel frowned. The FSU was the Firearms Support Unit, the armed branch of the police force for this area including Bromersley. He couldn't begin to imagine what they needed to phone him about. He forgot all about Harker. 'What do *they* want?'

'Don't know, sir.'

He reached his office and picked up the phone.

'DS Jock Keene here, sir. Sorry to bother you, but you haven't been to the small arms range for almost six months now. I thought you would want to be reminded. I expect you want to maintain your certification.'

Angel's mouth dropped open. Wow! This was important. He certainly did. He mustn't lose his licence to carry a handgun.

While use of firearms in the Bromersley force was normally entirely in the hands of the FSU at Wakefield, there were certain specified circumstances when suitably trained policemen and women might be armed. Angel wanted to be certain that he would be among the ones authorized.

'Oh yes, Jock, indeed I do.'

'Well, you need to get practice time in and six bulls before the twenty-first. That only gives you today or tomorrow, and I can't do you tomorrow because I've fourteen rookies to get through.'

'Today?' he said and rubbed his chin. There was such a lot pending. He liked firing a gun on the practice range. It was relaxing. The change would do him good, and he must retain his licence at all costs.

'Two o'clock looks good, sir.'

CHAPTER FOUR

It was five minutes to two.

Angel found a parking space in the police yard in Wakefield and drove the BMW into it. He reported to reception, proved his identity, waited for the clerk to make a phone call, then he was escorted outside the building by a uniformed PC. They walked through the car park, passed two new red-brick buildings which were dedicated to the selection, training and veterinary services of police dogs, then across another parking area packed with police vehicles including specialized transporters for police horses and 4 x 4 Range Rovers with close netting across the windows ready for use in riot situations. They reached an isolated windowless building with iron doors. It had 'No Parking' signs all the way round it. The PC rang the bell then both of them looked directly sideways to the right. There were no buildings, telegraph poles or trees for several hundred yards, but they both knew there was a camera out there somewhere, with a super-duper extra-powerful lens.

After a few moments, there was a clang, the iron door was released and they made their way through it, pulling it shut behind them.

There were two doors inside. One had the word 'Armoury' on the door and the other the words 'Small Arms Range'.

The PC went through the right-hand door then into an office.

DS Keene was at a desk. He stood up and nodded at Angel. The PC handed Angel over to Keene as if he was delivering a parcel. He produced a chitty which Keene signed, then he went out.

'Glad you made it, sir. Can't have you unlicensed,' Keene said. 'I'll get you kitted out straightaway.'

'Thank you, Jock,' Angel said, looking round. He was surprised to discover that he was nervous even though he had been through this routine many times and almost always passed first time. Thoughts about his eyesight were at the back of his mind. He had never thought he needed spectacles but that requirement with age came to many people.

Keene went through a steel-barred door to the other side of the office and came out carrying a pistol, a box of rounds and two pairs of ear protectors. He crossed in front of Angel and said, 'Right, sir. I've got everything. Come on through.'

Angel said nothing and followed him out of the office door into a short passageway, then through another door into darkness. He heard the click of switches and a powerful floodlight illuminated the nearest part of the range.

Twenty-five yards down the range, in a row, were six life-size wooden cut-outs of men in silhouette, numbered one to six, with bullseye targets painted on the head, chest, forearm and leg.

Keene put a Glock G17 hand pistol, a box of fifty rounds of ammunition and two pairs of ear protectors on the counter rail facing the target and moved about a yard away to Angel's left and behind him.

Then he said: 'In your own time, load.'

Angel put on the ear protectors, picked up the pistol and squeezed the handgrip. It felt good. He knew that Keene was watching him and would be marking him for the confidence and dexterity he showed in handling the gun, in loading the magazine, as well as his skill at hitting the targets. He didn't want to fluff anything.

He knew of a fellow officer who had been refused a licence because in the course of loading a magazine he had knocked an open box of rounds off the counter rail and they had rolled round the floor. The examiner had good reason; he said that in the time it took to pick up the rounds, fill the magazine and load the gun, he could have been shot twenty times. Angel didn't intend to be the victim of any of his own carelessness.

He gripped the pistol securely by the barrel and pressed the catch at the bottom of the handgrip to release the magazine. He carefully loaded it with seventeen rounds. He had counted them. He knew it was the maximum the magazine would hold. He pushed the magazine back into the handgrip until he heard and felt it click, then he placed the loaded gun down on the rail, muzzle facing the target, and put his hands down by his sides.

'Gun ready,' he said.

'Now remember, sir, using number one target lane. You need to hit at least six consecutive bullseyes to pass. Also you must use all four targets in descending sequence. Starting with the head, then the chest, then the arm, the leg and then back to the head again. And give me time to call out the result of each shot before you fire again. All right?'

'Yes. Right,' Angel said and put on a pair of the ear protectors.

Keene leaned forward, picked up the other pair, set them on his head then said, 'In your own time, beginning at the top target, *fire*.'

Angel picked up the gun, gripped it tight, held it out in front, aimed it at the top target and squeezed the trigger. The gunshot echoed round the building. His hand jerked back and up.

Keene looked at the target through a pair of binoculars and said, 'That's an outer.'

Angel pulled a face, readjusted his hold on the handgrip, steadied his aim and fired again.

'An inner,' Keene said.

It was still not good enough. Angel fired again.

'Bullseye,' Keene said.

And again.

'Bullseye.' And again. 'Bullseye.' And it went on. 'Bullseye. Bullseye. Bullseye. Bullseye. Bullseye. Cease firing. That's your six, sir. More than six. That's great. Cease firing. *Cease firing!*'

But Angel kept pulling the trigger. And again. And again. And again.

'*Cease firing!*' Keene yelled louder, then he leaned forward and put his hand on Angel's wrist, the wrist holding the gun. Angel stopped firing and looked round at him.

'Cease firing,' Keene said. 'Didn't you hear me? Cease firing. You must stop firing when I give you the command "Cease fire". Anyway, you've got your licence.'

Angel sighed. He'd got his licence. That was great.

'Sorry,' he said as he took off his ear protectors. 'I must not have heard you.'

He put the gun on the rail in front of him. Keene didn't believe him. He peered closely into his eyes as he turned away.

Angel had heard him all right, but for some reason he had wanted to keep on firing. He had enjoyed pulling that trigger, hitting bullseyes and seeing the targets move as the lead hit them. He could happily have gone on and emptied the magazine.

'*Unload*,' Keene said. 'And put the unused rounds back in the box.'

As Angel removed the magazine and began the process of emptying it, Keene said, 'Something bothering you, sir? Are you on edge about something? It's a bit of a strain being a copper these days, especially in the investigating branch.'

Angel looked at him and smiled.

'And it's getting tougher,' Keene said. 'I know that in Bromersley you've got that Manchester mob at your heels. Is that it?'

Angel frowned. 'What do you mean, Jock? What Manchester mob?'

He gave him a knowing look and touched his nose with his forefinger. 'If it's hush-hush, sir, that's all right by me. I understand.'

'No. No. It's not hush-hush. I don't know what are you talking about. What Manchester mob? Tell me.'

'The Corbetts. James and Lloyd Corbett.'

Angel blinked, then his eyes wandered from side to side beneath half-closed lids. He carried on pushing rounds out of the magazine into the box. 'Yes. I know of them. What about them?'

'A couple of hard men. I had two Lancashire lads from Preston, or somewhere round there, I think, they were. They'd had one of Corbett's men through their hands a little while back… They understood that the brothers felt that their faces were getting too well known in Manchester and that side of the Pennines, so they had been making sorties into Yorkshire to see if there were any easy pickings, and they seemed to be getting comfortable in Bromersley. Well, knowing you and DI Asquith, and Ron Gawber and Trevor Crisp, I naturally wondered how you were getting along with them on your patch.'

Angel pursed his lips then said, 'Who were these lads, Jock?'

'Don't know, sir. A couple of bobbies from out there, Preston or Blackburn or a little place, might have been Bamber Bridge. Can't remember. It's a bit since now. A lot of people pass through here in the course of a week.'

'I'll have to keep my eyes open, Jock. James and Lloyd Corbett, eh? I've certainly heard of them.'

'They're nasty people, sir. Be very careful. They have no respect for human life. None at all.'

Angel's lips tightened across his teeth.

'You wanted me, sir,' Ahmed said.

'Come in,' Angel said. 'Close the door. Sit down. On the PNC, there are a couple of characters, James Corbett and Lloyd Corbett — brothers. You'll easily find them. They began their nefarious activities in Manchester. I don't know where you would find them these days. I want you to pull off a photograph of each of them, head and shoulders, front view...both to fit an A4 sheet. Here is the text to go with them. I want you to make up a "Wanted" poster.'

Ahmed leaned forward. It was something interesting to do. He did a lot of updating of files, which was exacting and boring. 'How many do you want, sir?'

Angel was considering the number when the phone rang. He reached out for it.

'A hundred should do it,' he said, then into the phone he said, 'Angel.'

It was a young constable on reception.

'Sorry to bother you, sir. There's a woman up here asking to see somebody in charge. And I don't quite know —'

Angel's jaw muscles tightened. 'Well, put her on to the super. That's the procedure. I'm busy at the moment.'

'The super's out, sir. So is Inspector Asquith. You're the only one left.'

Angel squeezed the handset. 'What does she want? Can't *you* deal with it?'

'She wouldn't talk to me, sir. She's a bit...difficult. Come up from Surrey today specially, she says. Rather posh. Says it's a matter of life or death.'

At that, Angel knew he would have to see her.

'All right. Tell the lady I won't keep her a moment.'

'Right, sir,' the young PC said. 'Thank you, sir.' He sounded relieved.

Angel shook his head and replaced the phone. He wasn't pleased. He turned to Ahmed. 'Nip up to reception. There's a lady to see me. Bring her down to me in here.'

'Right, sir,' he said and rushed off.

Angel hardly had time to glance at the post on his desk when Ahmed arrived back, knocked on the door and showed the lady in.

Angel stood up to greet her. He liked what he saw. He guessed she was in her forties. He took in her short blonde hair, smart navy suit, long legs and huge solitaire diamond on the third finger of her left hand.

'Please sit down,' he said, and he turned to Ahmed and nodded towards the door.

Ahmed went out.

The lady remained standing.

'Forgive me,' she said, 'but I really need to see someone more senior. I understand you are only an inspector.'

She had a pleasant, deep voice. Probably smoked twenty a day.

'That's right,' he said, 'and I'm sorry, but I'm as senior as you can get here today. Everybody else is away. Inspector Angel is my name. Perhaps you would like to start by telling me *your* name and address, and then tell me how I might assist you.'

She looked at him thoughtfully. He pointed at the chair. She glanced at it briefly, considered it for a moment then sat down. She looked back across the desk at him; put her handbag on her knee without looking at it.

Angel sat there poised with a pen over a used envelope he had taken out of his inside pocket.

'Inspector Angel,' she said thoughtfully.

He looked up.

'Inspector Angel,' she repeated.

'That's right,' he said.

'Do you know, I may have heard of you. Are you the same Inspector Angel who they say has a hundred per cent success record in solving murder cases?'

He frowned, licked his lips then said, 'Yes. I suppose it is me.'

Her face changed. She smiled briefly. She put her handbag on the floor and wriggled in the chair. 'I've read about you in the papers. They say you can think like a murderer and that you've got a brain as fast as quicksilver.'

He swallowed. He didn't like those sort of comments. He didn't know how to respond. He wasn't very good with compliments. He could cope with most things, but he didn't have a ready answer for anything flattering.

'That's just so much newspaper twaddle,' he said with a wrinkle of the nose. 'Let's start with your name, please.'

'My name is Mrs Josephine Henderson. I am staying for one night at least at The Feathers Hotel on Bradford Road. But my home address is Five Trees, Larchfield Hill, Surrey. I have come about my sister Miss Selina Line. I am very worried about her. She lives with me there, well, she used to live there. She has been acting very strangely lately. She left abruptly on 31 July and I haven't seen her since. I am extremely fond of her. She is my younger sister and I feel responsible for her, and I believe she's in very great danger.'

'In what way?'

'Well, she's not very worldly. She's forty-four, not married, never had a...serious boyfriend, you know.'

Angel didn't know. He frowned. 'What was her work? What did she do?'

'She didn't work. She had no need to. Anyway, she wasn't allowed to. My late father, our late father, didn't want his daughters to work. He was Sir Gregory Line.'

Gregory Line? Sir Gregory Line? The name was familiar. To do with new buildings. In queer shapes. Won all those awards for designs in the eighties and nineties...died a couple of years ago.

'The architect?'

'Yes. My sister packed a suitcase and left almost three weeks ago, and, apart from a very short phone call from a telephone call box in Bromersley on 1 August and then another taken by my housekeeper yesterday, I haven't heard a word...and we were so close.'

'Please go on.'

Mrs Henderson looked away briefly then looked back. 'There was a...misunderstanding between a friend of hers and her. This triggered off a row between us. Well, it had happened a few times lately. There had been lots of rows. Too many. In fact, ever since Daddy died.'

She stopped talking and began looking down at her hands, both sides, finger by finger.

Angel waited. He said nothing.

'She…she latched herself on to people, Inspector. The most unlikely people. For instance, there was the man who delivered the Christmas tree last Christmas. She let him into the house, told him where we wanted the tree putting in the hall. He hadn't been in the house an hour and she had found out he wasn't married and she had got him to take her to the theatre the following Saturday.'

'Was it a success? Did she enjoy the trip?'

'I didn't know about it until afterwards. She *said* she had enjoyed it, but, fortunately, the relationship didn't go any further. But there were more…cases. There was the man from the security firm who came to sell us an updated system. Another man she met in the library, who helped her with the new automatic machinery. I can't imagine what she had said to him, but she got invited to his house and had a meal with him *and* his wife. She came home in a flood of tears. Fortunately, these…adventures were short lived.'

Angel pursed his lips. He could see the pattern. 'Well, what caused your sister to leave the house the last time?'

'The last man proved to be very difficult. She said that she thought she would like to get in trim after Christmas. She saw an ad in the local paper, interviewed a man, a so-called personal trainer, and engaged him to come to the house two afternoons a week. He was a very personable young man. In his twenties. Prime physique. Suntanned. Dark hair. Blue eyes. I saw him arrive in his shorts. I could see that this was a potentially volatile situation. So I thought that I would join in the sessions to keep a sisterly eye on things. Selina wasn't pleased but she tolerated my presence. Anyway, she had three exercise sessions and after that they're talking on the phone late at night, making arrangements to meet somewhere. The next day I got a phone call from a young woman crying her eyes out because she had found out that Selina was coming between her and her partner. And that she was expecting *their* second child! Oh dear. I had to put the poor girl right and then explain all this to Selina. At first she didn't believe me, thought I was making it up, just to separate them. Anyway she saw the muscle man — who, of course, lied at first and she believed him. Anyway, it all came out, although it took a few days. There were a lot of upsets, tears and unhappiness. Poor Selina. It was a mess. You would have thought she would have been grateful to me, but no, I think she hated me. She stayed in her bedroom all the next day and the day after that…wouldn't speak to me. I tried to speak to her. All she would say was "go away". I went out riding. It always relaxes me. I was out all the afternoon. When I got back, I went up to try to make peace with her again but was met on the stairs by our housekeeper who told me Selina had gone out of the house dressed up to the nines carrying two suitcases. Apparently she had called for a taxi, which was unusual in itself. Our gardener handyman would have taken her anywhere she had wanted to go in our 4 x 4. Anyway, I was devastated. I had no idea where she had gone. She didn't return that night. She's been gone nineteen nights, and that big lumbering house is too big for one person, Inspector.'

'I assumed you were married, Mrs Henderson?'

'I was. My husband died four years ago.'

'I'm sorry. But she did contact you?'

'A very brief starchy phone call the following morning. She said that she had met a schoolteacher called Harry, that he was a widower, that they were madly in love, that he definitely wasn't married, and that they were getting married a week on Saturday, and that I wasn't to try and stop her, and that was all. She was very emotional and she wasn't that clear but that was the essence of the call. She didn't say that she loved me or anything like that. She didn't wait for me to say anything. I immediately had the phone call traced by the telephone company and discovered that it was from a call box on Victoria Road in Bromersley in South Yorkshire.'

Angel raised his head. 'How very enterprising of you, Mrs Henderson.'

'It is one of the perks of being the daughter of a knight of the realm, Inspector. The title impresses some people.'

'And that's what brought you here?'

'Yes. Now, can you please find her for me? She is extremely wealthy in her own right. I fear for her safety. I think she is in the hands of someone very unscrupulous. She is very naive still.'

'There is nothing illegal about two single people getting married.'

Her eyes narrowed, her bottom lip quivered. 'There's more, Inspector, much more. She had a large sum on deposit at the Egham, Epsom and Esher Building Society. The manager told me this morning that yesterday she had withdrawn every penny of it. Also, she had several thousand pounds in her ordinary bank account. That has also been withdrawn in cash in their branch here and the account closed. I rushed into her bedroom, and looked in her dressing-table drawer. She has taken all her jewellery. The stuff that was Grandmother's, that she had inherited, the Cranberry garnet earrings, the emerald and diamond necklace, and the eight-carat solitaire diamond ring that Daddy gave her on her eighteenth birthday. It made me shudder when I thought about it. I fear that she is in the hands of some crook who is taking as much money from her as he can and then he's going to murder her. I immediately packed a bag, caught the train and here I am. You must find her, Inspector, before it is too late.'

CHAPTER FIVE

Angel arrived at his office as usual at 0828 hours, picked up the phone and tapped in a number.

Ahmed answered. 'Good morning, sir.'

'Good morning. Get a message out to Ron Gawber and Trevor Crisp that I want them in my office, ASAP. All right? And when you've done that, I want you in here, promptly.'

A few moments later, Ahmed knocked on the door and pushed it open. 'They're on their way, sir.'

Angel picked up the wedge of A4 sheets with pictures and descriptions of James and Lloyd Corbett made up like nineteenth-century posters of wanted outlaws from off the desk, waved them at him then dropped them down with a bang. 'They're great, Ahmed. Just what I wanted.'

The young man smiled.

'Now I want you to get a list of public houses licensed in the Bromersley area from the desk sergeant and note down the name of the licensee. Then I want you to deliver personally one of these posters into the hand of every licensee and get a signature from him or her for it. I want you to say that DI Angel of Bromersley Police sends his compliments and requests their cooperation in the event of them seeing either of these two men. Got it?'

'Yes, sir.'

'Take Scrivens with you. It shouldn't take you two more than a day if you take the area car.'

Ahmed smiled. That was a job he would enjoy. He liked to get out of the office.

Angel picked up the leaflets, took one off the top and handed the rest to Ahmed, who quickly took them and made for the door.

The door closed. Angel watched it and smiled.

Almost immediately, DS Gawber and DS Crisp arrived.

He went swiftly through all the facts he had gleaned from Mrs Henderson the previous afternoon about her missing sister, Selina Line.

Gawber said: 'Isn't this simply a missing person inquiry, sir?'

'It might be, Ron. But there is such a lot of money and jewellery involved, which is worrying. Also this particular woman sounded very vulnerable — no mother, and two years after her father died, she may have felt lonely. Her sister said she was unmarried and unworldly. Also, the crook wouldn't dare simply to abandon her after he'd picked her clean. She has seen him, his place of residence...she has lived with him. She would be able to give a very detailed description of him, and if he had a record, she'd pick him out on the PNC in a minute.'

Angel looked at both sergeants. They exchanged glances with each other and then nodded soulfully. The outlook cast a quiet and sombre gloom over the gathering, but also brought with it a sense of urgency.

'Do we have any pictures of her, sir?' Gawber said.

'Mrs Henderson is having some photographs of her sent forthwith from her home. She's also having some photographs of the missing jewellery forwarded from the insurance company. She is staying for the time being at The Feathers, she says, to keep close to the search.'

Angel looked at Crisp. 'Now I want *you* to enquire at the registrar's office for details of a wedding that took place in Bromersley, according to Mrs Henderson, on Saturday, ninth of this month, between a man called Harry something or other, a widower, he said, and Selina Line. I suppose she wouldn't change her name. Anyway, see if you can find it.'

'Was it a church service or a civil service?' Crisp said.

'I've no idea. That's something you've got to find out.'

'Might it be a bigamous marriage, sir?'

Angel's fists tightened. 'It might. It might. It might not. Find out. Go on. Crack on with it.'

'Right, sir,' he said and went out.

Angel looked at Gawber. 'She said the bridegroom was a teacher, Ron, a widower. Not much to go on. A teacher with a first name of Harry. Schools are on holiday. You'll have to start at the education office in the town hall. See what you can dig up.'

'Right, sir.'

Gawber went out and closed the door.

Angel stood up, then walked purposefully up the corridor to the security door and out of the station. He bounced down the steps, turned right at the bottom and walked on 200 yards or so to the magistrates' court, then turned right and through the door marked 'Probation Office'. He passed the 'Reception and Waiting Room' door and stepped smartly along the corridor to an old black door, where he tapped gently on one of the panels.

After a few seconds a young woman with long black undisciplined hair opened the door six inches and peered round it.

He smiled at her. 'Marie, have you a minute?'

'Oh,' she said in a quiet voice. 'I'm with a client, Michael, but I'll only be five minutes.'

He nodded.

She closed the door.

He leaned back against the wall, folded his arms and waited. Waiting wasn't easy for him. Five minutes is a long time when you have a lot to do and a woman's life might be in danger.

The time ticked away, and the probation officer duly opened her private door and let him in.

'Who are you looking for this time?' she said.

She was used to Angel coming in armed with an almost impossible description.

'Simple, Marie,' he said. 'I'm looking for a man called Harry, who is a schoolteacher, a widower and who has been free for at least the past nineteen days.'

Her eyebrows shot up. 'If he's still a schoolteacher, he won't be on the books.'

He frowned. It was true. Education authorities don't let crooks anywhere near schools.

'Maybe he had *been* a schoolteacher?' he said.

She shrugged. 'Maybe he hadn't?'

He rubbed his chin.

'Maybe your man hasn't even a record?' she said.

Angel thought quickly and said: 'Maybe he got the job through forging his references?'

'You're stubborn.'

'I have to be.'

'How do you know he's supposed to be a schoolteacher?'

'A witness said so.'

'How does the witness know?'

'The missing woman, her sister, told her.'

Marie's jaw dropped. She saw that this was serious. 'An abduction?'

'Might be,' he said.

He didn't add his private thoughts. An abduction was ghastly enough.

'Is that all you know?' she said.

His lips tightened against his teeth. 'That's all the witness, the woman's sister, knows,' he said. Then in a quiet, cold voice he said, 'I believe he lives somewhere not far from the phone box on Victoria Road. And if I was doing a profile, I'd say he was tolerably physically attractive to the mature woman, probably tall, over forty, a great talker, confidence trickster and…' he added heavily, 'And a murderer.'

He could hear the phone in his office ringing out when he was halfway down the green corridor. He wondered if it was Marie from the probation office. He began to run. She had not been able to suggest any of her clients that filled his spec off the top of her head while he had been with her. He wondered if she had suddenly thought of somebody. He pushed open the office door, reached over the desk and snatched up the handset.

It was Sir Max Monro's housekeeper, dear Mrs Dunleavy. She sounded very worried.

'I wondered if you heard anything from Mr Nigel, Inspector. I really need some instructions about the house, you know. I really would like to get back to living in my own house. Also there is a lot of post backing up here addressed to him. And there are bills rolling in for the house which will need paying. I can't pay them. There are lots of inquiries for Mr Nigel and not all friendly. I had a man here yesterday wanting to issue Mr Nigel with a writ. He thought I was protecting him, you know...that I knew where he was. Wanted to look round the house, value the furniture. I had a job to keep him out. Good job I had the door on the chain.'

Angel was quite perturbed. 'I have heard nothing, Mrs Dunleavy,' he said. 'But you mustn't worry about a thing. It is a job for Sir Max's solicitor, the man who drew up the Will. He was at the funeral. Contact him. Tell him what you want to do and do it. If you have any difficulty, let me know.'

There was a heavy sigh. 'Oh, thank you, Inspector. Thank you very much. And you think that will be all right?'

'I'm certain of it.'

There was another heavy sigh. 'Oh, thank you, Inspector. I will phone him immediately.' Then she said: 'Are you having any success finding that...that ruby stone?'

'Not yet. It is rather difficult in the absence of Nigel. When he turns up, will you let me know?'

'I certainly will,' she said.

The call ended, leaving Mrs Dunleavy a happy woman, but it had reminded Angel that he really ought to visit the convent in North Yorkshire. It was still possible that there was somebody or something there that might lead him to Princess Yasmin. He must find her, see that she knows the facts and is made aware of her inheritance. It wouldn't be easy. Harker had given him specific orders not to spend any time on that case. He was still chasing him for a result on the assault on the four men in The Feathers.

The phone rang again. It was Harker. Angel smiled wryly at the coincidence. He thought his ears must have been burning.

'I've just had a call from the hospital,' Harker snapped. 'Get over there smartly. Charles Drumme was admitted at 7.30 this morning. He has a gunshot wound.'

Angel's head came up. He blinked and charged out of the office. Time might be important. Drumme might have something to say about who had shot him.

Drumme was the king of crime in Bromersley and had held that position since Caleb Hull had been put away for eight years in 2005, mainly the result of assiduous investigative work by Angel. His arrest had slashed the crime figures for minor offences overnight. That day there had been a spirit of celebration in the station. After the sentence, the chief constable had called him up to his office and congratulated him.

Drumme was a nasty character, and he held the gaming machine franchise in most of Bromersley's pubs and hotels, had a string of girls working for him down by the canal and ran a patchy protection racket involving some of the small cafes, takeaway restaurants and several shops. Angel understood that the cost of the 'protection' was unspecified and unpredictable, but the result was that he and his gang usually ate well at no cost. The rackets were all built on fear. Fear of having a face slashed or property trashed. Angel could never get a witness to speak against him and his small band of thugs.

Angel reached the hospital in eight minutes, enquired at reception for Drumme's ward number, took the lift to the fourth floor, made his way to the nurses' station and was instantly directed to room 12 opposite. The room door was wide open. As he approached, he saw that it was a single ward and that the patient was purple-faced and propped in a sitting position with pillows. He had a plaster over one eye, a surgical dressing on his tanned chest and a thick bandage round one arm above the elbow. A plastic bag of clear liquid hung from a stand with a pipe flowing down to his wrist. Even so, Angel knew it was Charles Drumme. Their eyes met. He recognized Angel. His eyes flashed and his lips tightened and curled with anger.

'You're too bloody soon, Angel,' Drumme said. 'My funeral's not for another thirty years at least.'

'By the colour of your face, and all those bandages, I should watch it. It could be sooner than you think.' He reached for the chair by the wall, pulled it across and sat down.

'You needn't make yourself comfortable, Angel. This isn't one of your interview rooms. One word from me and these nurses'll have you out of this ward and down that corridor quicker than you can say "Let's be having you".'

'There's no cause to be difficult, Charlie. This is only a friendly call.'

'The name's Charles, and I'm not difficult. Where's the fags and the Glenfiddich? If this was a friendly call I wouldn't expect you to come empty handed.'

'Don't push the smart chat, Charles. I heard you'd been injured. Naturally we're always concerned if one of our… regular customers gets duffed up.'

'There was no fight. I walked into a door, that's all.'

'What about the gunshot wound? Was it where you banged your arm accidentally on a projecting door key?'

'It's not a gunshot wound. The doctor made a mistake, that's all.'

Angel smiled wryly and wiped a hand across his mouth. 'Who did it, Charles?'

'Forget it, Angel. Move on.'

Angel leaned forward. 'If you finger him and we can prove it, he'd get five years. He's very likely still got powder burns on him as we speak. Do yourself a favour. Get him out of the way. He can't be a friend of yours, Charles. Just give me a name. I can have him picked up and put away before he gets to you again.'

'Forget it, Angel. I settle my own scores.'

'Yes, and that's the trouble. Innocent people get hurt. And you could go inside for it. At least if I do it, it's legal. It's done properly, with no comebacks.'

'Buzz off.'

'You're a fool.'

'You don't know what you're talking about. You've no idea who they were.'

'They certainly made a monkey out of you.'

'You know nothing. I was caught unprepared, that's all. It won't happen again. I got my methods.'

'They must have been outsiders, eh, Charlie? Local heavies would have been a bit wary of you. They must have been from another patch?'

'No comment.'

'Don't come the "no comment" with me, Charlie. They *were*, weren't they?'

Drumme's eyes flashed angrily. His jaw stiffened and his lips curled cruelly. He strained both arms and legs to try to raise himself up. 'It's *Charles*,' he bawled and then flopped back on the bed with a pained expression. If he could have gotten out of bed he would have done. 'And I'll say anything I frigging well want to. Now get the hell out of here.'

'All right. All right. Say who did this to you and I'll go right now and lock them up.'

'Buzz off. I'm a patient in here. I have rights. I don't have to put up with the likes of you. You're a frigging nuisance. I'm telling you nothing. I never tell coppers anything. You know that. Now, buzz off and don't come back.'

Angel rubbed his chin. He stood up. He put the chair back by the wall. His eyes suddenly twinkled mischievously.

'I can see I'm breaking your resistance down, Charlie, but you're tired,' he said. 'I'll come back and have another word with you later.' He turned to go.

'Don't frigging bother!' Drumme screamed, and a stainless-steel kidney bowl and a plastic jug of water followed him out of the room, landing noisily on the corridor floor.

CHAPTER SIX

Angel came out of the hospital through the revolving door in reflective mood. It had almost been a waste of time. Detectives would give up interviewing if interviewees were all like Charles Drumme. Reading between the lines, all that he had deduced was that Drumme had been attacked by outsiders, people he didn't know, which probably meant the Corbetts.

He looked among the sea of cars for the BMW. He recognized the roof and made his way past a parked ambulance and a taxi towards it.

He was thinking he could do without the Corbetts on his patch. Then he heard the ringing of his mobile phone. He dived into his pocket. It was Superintendent Harker. He sounded in a state.

'Where the hell are you?' he bawled. 'We've got an armed robbery in progress. It's on Market Street. A Pelican Security van. I've informed the FSU. Set up roadblocks on Bradford Road and Sheffield Road. Market Street is a one-way street. You can't get behind them because they've blocked it off with a stolen furniture-type van of some sort. I'm on my way down there now. Meet me at the exit end of Market Street ASAP.'

There was a click and that was it.

Angel ran to his car, reversed out of the parking bay, worked his way along the parking lanes and eventually on to the main road. He raced down Park Road. He knew exactly the quickest way to the end of Market Street. He drove quickly and carefully, overtaking everything when it was safe to do so. He switched on the RT so that he could hear any reports that might come in to the operations room. It was going to take him another two minutes to get on to Victoria Road, which led to the end of Market Street. The robbers surely would be clear of the scene by the time he arrived there. The blocking off the street behind them was, from their point of view, a smart ploy. The operation sounded like the work of a sophisticated gang.

There was a lot of chatter on the RT from traffic division about traffic delays and a broken-down car at the traffic lights on Sheffield Road. Then he heard something about the robbery. It was an exchange between the sergeant in the operations room to Inspector Asquith, who was also on his way to the scene.

'There were two vehicles involved. A red van and a green van seen being driven away. At least three armed men and a woman in balaclavas. No shots fired, but a big explosion and smoke from the back of the Pelican Security van, doors blown off in the street, money cage opened with heavy wire cutters, and van emptied of a quantity of canvas sacks and transferred to robbers' vans, now driven away. A woman in a flat over a baker's shop had a bird's eye view of the crime scene and has been giving a commentary to the sergeant in the operations room.'

Angel was on Victoria Road. A small car in front was driving close to the kerb and then out again, then in. Probably looking for somewhere to park. Angel let out a long hard blast on the car horn. The car stopped dead. He quickly changed down to second gear, pressed hard down on the accelerator and drove round in front of it. The driver glared at him, shook his fist and yelled something obscene. Angel ignored him and drove on.

The end of Market Street was in sight. He could see the McDonald's sign on the corner. A bus was ahead of him. He stuck his nose round the rear of it and saw a green van careen round the corner on two wheels; the tyres squealed and pedestrians stared at it. Then it straightened up. It had come out of Market Street. His pulse raced. If he could follow it, without being spotted… It was green as described. It was being driven very quickly. He latched on to it as it weaved in and around the busy town traffic. He gripped the steering wheel determinedly. He was not intending to lose it. He would stick with it. He'd follow it to hell if that's where it was going. It was being driven far more quickly than was safe. It turned out of the town on to the ring road. Angel was close behind. It seemed to be making for the Ml. He would have liked to have phoned in for support or reported his position but the speed of travelling needed all his attention. He wasn't going to risk losing it. It took corners on two wheels. Even on the straight, when it wandered too close to the kerb or the central white line, it was jerkily corrected at the very last moment.

The driver had shown no signs of acknowledging that he was being followed. Angel considered overtaking the van. His BMW would easily do that. But they were armed and he wasn't, so that idea was quashed. The van reached the roundabout incorporating the slip roads to the M1 but the driver kept in the offside lane. The van went round the roundabout all the way. He stayed right behind them. He became uneasy, but he had no choice. They made the circle again. Angel's face dropped. He had been sussed. They had used that ploy to find out if he had been following them. They now knew that he had. His pulse raced; he didn't know what they would do. Next time round, unexpectedly, the van moved left into the nearside lane and went down the narrow slip road. At the same time, the back doors of the van opened and a man dressed in black and wearing a balaclava threw several handfuls of something too small to identify.

Angel was wary. He braked and dropped back a little. Then he heard a bang. It was a puncture. His steering was heavy and uncontrollable. He braked. There were three more bangs in quick succession. The BMW slewed across the slip road out of Angel's control. He saw the man hanging out of the back of the van wave mockingly as the van pulled away and got smaller and smaller and filtered neatly into the traffic on the motorway ahead as the BMW came to a stop.

Superintendent Harker stood in his office, hands on hips, his face redder than a judge's vest. 'I told you to rendezvous at the end of Market Street.'

'When I saw the green van come out at speed, I thought it too good an opportunity to miss.'

Harker sniffed. 'But you didn't *do* anything. You didn't *see* anything. Just knocked up a bill to recover your car and repair four punctures.'

Angel stood there, with nothing to say. Then he remembered. 'I got the van's index number, sir.'

Harker glared at him. 'So did everybody else. You didn't even call in and tell me or anybody where you were, to give us chance to head the robbers off or put up a roadblock.'

Angel looked down briefly. It was true, but it had been virtually impossible to use a phone. 'I was travelling too fast keeping up with the van, sir.'

Harker pulled a face like he'd just sampled prison hooch. 'I am not going to ask if you travelled at speeds exceeding the speed limit.'

Angel rubbed his chin. There was no answer to that.

Harker sat down in the swivel chair. He opened and closed a drawer in his desk several times, eventually closing it with a particularly loud bang.

'You'd better get back to finding out why visitors staying at the best hotel in town get their fingers smashed in the middle of the night,' he said. 'We don't want a repeat of that sort of thing. Gets the town a bad name. You're supposed to be the wonder boy detective. You get all the headlines. It's time you had that little mystery solved. Should be as easy as pie to a hotshot detective like you.'

Angel's head came up. A hot sensation generated across his chest and swelled up into his face. He wanted to give Harker a mouthful in retaliation, but his desire to remain in the force was even stronger.

'Go on,' Harker said with a gesture of dismissal. 'Get on with it. Be sure to tell Asquith what happened.'

Angel clenched his fists, nodded, walked out and closed the door.

If there had been a backside to kick, he would have kicked it. He stormed up to his room, went inside and slumped down at his desk. He frowned. Asquith? Haydn Asquith? He was the inspector in uniformed division on traffic. He looked great in the uniform. But he had had no experience in detecting techniques.

*

'Good morning, sir.'

'Good morning. Did you finish distributing those "Wanted" leaflets?'

'Yes, sir,' Ahmed said. 'I've brought the few that were left over.' He placed a folder on the desk.

'Great stuff. Did you notice if any of the licensees recognized either of the two men?' Angel asked.

'Didn't see any reaction, sir.'

He wrinkled his nose. 'Mmm. Right. Sit down a minute. I've got another job for you.'

Ahmed's face brightened. Anything that made a change from filing and downloading would be welcome.

'That case of the four men who were assaulted at The Feathers on the 23/24 June,' Angel said. 'We have made no progress whatsoever.'

Ahmed nodded and took out his notebook and pen.

'Now there has to be a link,' Angel said. 'There must be a relationship, a reason *why* those four men were attacked, and particularly why they were attacked in the same way. It couldn't possibly have happened randomly. The attacker went deliberately for the middle finger of the right hand of each man quite specifically. I don't know if it was a warning to each of them or what. I don't know if it was the stupid requirement sign of a club of some sort, or part of a crazy initiation service. Anyway, that link can only be determined by making comparisons, and there doesn't seem to be an in-house template for this. So I want you to devote yourself exclusively to it, and I want you to do it quickly. There isn't much time. I want you to create a table. Do it on the computer. It will need to be a very long list, with five columns, one for the question and one each for the answers of the four men. Now when you get four answers that are the same, then *there* will surely be the explanation of the assault. Right?'

'Yes, sir.'

'DS Gawber has the files. Get them from him. You'll get the answers from the most obvious questions asked when the men were interviewed in June. Start the table with those questions, such as age, marital status, nationality, home address. Inquire why they were staying in Bromersley that particular night. Put down what each man does for a living. Any police record? Does he drive a car? What make is it? And so on. Got the idea?'

'Yes, sir.'

'I know that there was absolutely nothing helpful about *those* particular answers, because I've already looked closely at them, but start there, and ask the victims more intrusive questions. You will have to speak to them individually on the phone. Interview the four again and continue with the questions. Keep with it until you find the question that produces four identical answers, and then you will have solved it. It's time-consuming, but it's the only way.'

Ahmed stood up. 'Right, sir,' he said, looking eager to begin. 'But wouldn't you think the four men themselves would know why they were attacked in that way?'

'They say they don't know,' Angel said. 'They say they haven't a clue. In fact, they'd like to find out the reason themselves and I understand that.'

Ahmed nodded then said, 'And they say they didn't know each other, sir, before the attacks?'

The phone rang.

'They say not,' Angel said as he reached out for the handset. Then he pointed at the door with his thumb. 'Now hop off and get on with it. I am up to my eyes.'

Ahmed went swiftly out and closed the door.

It was Marie from the probation office on the phone.

'I haven't got a Harry in the whole of the town,' she said. 'No schoolteachers or ex-schoolteachers. No widowers. But there have been and are lots of ex-offenders who were footloose and fancy-free on 31 July and still are.'

Angel shook his head. 'You're a big disappointment to me, Marie.'

'What makes you think you're looking for an ex-offender?'

'I have to start somewhere. I have so little to go on. The woman missing is well off, *very* well off, never had a love-life, aged forty-four, sounds as plain as a bag of Be-Ro. She's just ripe for plucking by an experienced crook, and is almost certainly now picked clean and dumped. Her bank accounts have been emptied. Paid out in cash. There's absolutely no valid reason why she would need to do that. She's been murdered or is being held against her will for a ransom. The trouble with that is...nobody's had a ransom demand.'

There was a pause.

'I hope you're wrong,' she said. 'You said that the suspect is likely to live somewhere near the phone box on Victoria Road?'

'That's right.'

'Well, I've nobody living anywhere near there. I have a Laurence Potter. Aged fifty. He's not a widower. Never been married. Lives on his own. Been in prison for burglary twice. Six months in 2001, and two years in 2005. He lives at 4 Creesforth Road. That's about half a mile from your phone box on Victoria Road. He's the nearest.'

He wrinkled his nose. 'Oh dear,' he said. 'Anybody else?'

'Don't be so ungracious, Michael. I am doing my best.'

He grunted something unintelligible, then said, 'Sorry. What's he like?'

'A model client. Keeps all his appointments here. Never misses. Never late.'

'Employed?'

'No. Like most of them.'

'The chap I'm looking for is supposed to be a schoolteacher. What's he look like? Is he attractive to women?'

'He doesn't do it for me, but he's pleasant enough.'

He made a note and said, 'Who else?'

'There's a man, Dennis Schuster. Aged sixty, looks younger. He's not a widower either, but he's been married, four times. Served two years for deception and fraud. Again, the only criteria of yours he fits is that he lives at 11 Edward Street...about a mile, I suppose, from the phone box, in the direction of the town centre. Well spoken. Now *he* could be a teacher.'

'And I suppose he's a model client too.'

'Yes. The mature, sensible ones — the ones who want to go straight — usually show me only their good side. It's their way of breaking away from you lot.'

He smiled wryly and shook his head even though she couldn't see him. 'Very wise, I'm sure,' he said. 'Is he in employment?'

'No.'

'Anybody else, Marie?'

'About a hundred, but you'll only grumble because they don't fit your criteria. Those two were not inside on 31 July, and they live closest to that phone box.'

He licked his lips. 'Thanks very much for all your efforts, Marie. I'll have a discreet look at them. I suppose that each of these is tolerably physically acceptable, tall, good head of hair, a great talker, a good liar and a cool murderer.'

Marie shuddered. 'I don't know, do I?'

*

The rain was heavy. It had been raining for the last few days on and off, but that morning it was coming down as if God had forgotten to turn off the tap. Local floods in the vulnerable places seemed predictable.

Angel went into Park Road post office, struggling with his umbrella, and joined the short queue up to the counter. As he stood there waiting, he selected several leaflets from the rack on the wall. When he reached the window, he bought a second-class stamp, returned to the BMW, put the stamp on to the dashboard shelf, tucked the leaflets into a clipboard he had borrowed from CID, and started the car. He turned left off Park Road on to Edward Street, a short street of small terraced houses, and pulled up to the kerbside outside number 3, which was four houses from the target house. Keeping the clipboard close to his chest, he walked quickly up to number 11 and knocked on the door. As he waited in the rain, he glanced through the official-looking post office leaflets and noticed that they were about the merits of borrowing money.

The door was soon opened by a young girl aged about ten. He shoved the leaflets back under the clip on the clipboard and smiled down at her. She glared back at him.

'Is your dad in, love?' Angel said.

She didn't answer. She turned round and said, 'Mam. There's a man here. Wants to know if me dad's in.'

'Who is it?' a voice said.

Angel said: 'Tell her I'm from the Nuway television programme.'

'He's from the no way —'

The woman appeared. Her hair was all over the place. 'What is it?' she said, pushing the girl inside.

Angel gave her his best George Clooney smile. 'Mrs Schuster?

'Yes. I'm Gloria Schuster.'

'I'm from Nuway Television. You will have heard of the programme Happy Families?'

'No,' she said, frowning.

He feigned surprise. He raised his eyebrows and said: 'Well, it's the quiz programme where the winners get £10,000 if they win and the runners-up get £2,000. They only have to answer five simple questions. Teams are chosen completely at random, but must consist of a man, his wife or partner and one child.'

'Ooooh; she said, her eyes shining. 'Excuse me a minute.' She turned and called out: 'Trudi! Go and tell your father I want him. He's on the bed reading the paper. Tell him it's *very important.*'

She turned back to Angel. Her face glowed. She began to stroke and pat her hair, trying to tidy it. 'Well,' she said, 'I used to be good at quizzes. I still do crosswords. This is very nice. Why did you choose us?'

He glanced at the clipboard. 'You *are* Mrs Dennis Schuster, aren't you?'

'Oh yes,' she said, running her hands down from her waist, smoothing the dress around her thighs.

'You have to attend the television recording studio in Leeds. You can manage that?'

'Oh, yes,' she said. 'We've got a car. We could certainly do with the money. My husband's unemployed at the moment. You said the teams are chosen at random?'

'Yes. The addresses come from head office,' he said quickly. He wanted to get another question in before the man Schuster arrived. 'You don't own or rent or use or have access to any other property, do you? Another house, an outhouse or garage...a building of any sort would earn you extra points.'

'No, just this house. But how does that work?'

He hadn't an answer. He was thinking on his feet. Thankfully, a man appeared in the doorway. 'You wanted me, darling?' He was tall, dark and slim with a voice like an actor. He looked Angel up and down. His eyes were all over.

Angel looked back at him.

Gloria Schuster said: 'Dennis, this man is from the television company —'

'The television show *Happy Families*, yes,' Angel said quickly. 'You win either £10,000 or £2,000.'

'I've not heard of it. Sounds very…interesting,' Schuster said in a bored, measured tone.

Angel saw the pupils of his eyes slide to one side then back again. When he had seen enough, he turned sideways, stuck a hand in his blazer pocket and struck a pose to show off his profile.

Angel's heartbeat increased. He could always spot an ex-con. This was a prime example. The man was unemployed, probably unemployable, and had served two years for deception and fraud. He conned an old lady out of her savings by pretending to be from the council and rendering free advice on investment. He originally got five years, it was such an extreme case of greed and heartlessness. It was reduced to three years on appeal, but he actually only served two years inside.

Now that Angel had seen him, he thought it highly probable that there were scores of other crimes committed by Schuster that had never been detected.

'Of course there are a few preliminary questions to be cleared,' Angel said. 'You are residents in the UK?'

'Of course,' he replied.

He saw Gloria smile, look at her husband then reach down and slip her hand in his.

'Always have your holidays together?' said Angel.

'Of course,' Schuster said.

'Does either of you have to travel in your line of work?'

'No.'

'Has either of you been away from the other — even for one night — over the past twelve months? To visit a relative, have a holiday, or whatever?'

'No. We always go everywhere together,' Gloria said.

Angel looked into Schuster's eyes. The man returned a practised steady gaze.

'Thank you very much,' Angel said. 'You fulfil all the criteria for inclusion in the show. I'll recommend you to the producers, and the company will write to you when they want you to come in. Good morning.'

He withdrew quickly into the rain before the Schusters began to ask difficult questions. He stepped lively to the BMW and drove rapidly out of Edward Street, leaving the couple energized but bemused.

As he turned back into Park Road to make his way to Creesforth Road, he thought over the interview he had had with the Schusters. His question to them about being away from home didn't necessarily elicit an honest answer. The point was that if Dennis Schuster had been the one to go through a marriage service with Selina Line, he would obviously have had to leave Gloria for some time afterwards to observe the ritual of the honeymoon. Schuster could hardly have avoided that. At the same time, Angel was reasonably satisfied that it was quite within Dennis Schuster's ability to have seduced Selina Line, gone through a marriage service with her, taken her money and then, presumably, murdered her. However, Angel was looking for somebody called Harry who was a schoolteacher. Schuster didn't fit the bill on either count.

Angel sighed and put his foot down on the accelerator. He still had another suspect to see. The notes Angel had on him from the PNC told him that Laurence Potter was fifty years of age, unmarried, and had been sent to prison for housebreaking twice: six months in 1999, and two years in 2001.

Angel headed purposefully to the other side of town, along Victoria Road, passing the phone box from where Selina Line had phoned her sister in Surrey. The road ran into Bradford Road and up to the church where he turned left on to Creesforth Road. It was at the old end of the road where the houses were much smaller and therefore much cheaper than further along. Potter lived at number 4, in a semi-detached house with the smallest of gardens. He noted that, as the probation officer had accurately said, Potter's house was about half a mile from the phone box on Victoria Road.

Armed with the clipboard, and umbrella, Angel opened the gate and walked down the path to the front door. He was about to press the doorbell when he heard a door open somewhere and a woman loudly call out.

'You devil, you,' she said. It was followed by a scream that turned into a roar of laughter.

He heard the door being closed, followed by the clickety-click of high-heeled shoes on wet flagstones. Then up the path at the side of the house came into view a slim, red-haired woman wearing more make-up than the cast of *Showboat*, and very little else. She was smiling and swinging a brown cardboard box by a string handle. It clearly didn't weigh much. The box had the words MERLIN VACUUM CLEANER printed on each side in big letters. She seemed totally unaware of the rain.

Their eyes met; she grinned and waved a hand at him.

He waved back while trying to memorize her face. He frowned as he identified the unsteady walk, the fixed smile and the wobble of the head. She was high on something.

He turned back to the front door and pressed the button push. It was some time before the door was unlocked. It was opened four inches on the chain. An eye peered through the gap.

'Yeah?'

Angel sensed this wasn't going to be as easy as the Schusters. He had to think of something that would interest the man and would be believable. 'I've called about your allocation of free vouchers for the lottery. It's Mr Potter, isn't it?'

'What?' he said. 'I don't know anything about it. I haven't applied for any.' He spoke slowly and his voice was slurred.

'You don't apply. They're allocated to you by the council, *if* you qualify.'

There was a pause.

A whiff of alcohol drifted through the gap. He reckoned that Potter was celebrating something.

Angel licked his bottom lip thoughtfully as he waited to see if he would take the bait.

'Not interested,' Potter eventually said. 'Stuff it,' he added, and began to close the door.

Angel thought quickly. 'Can *I* have your tickets then?' he said.

The door closed with a bang but reopened immediately with the chain off Potter pulled the door wide open and stood there, eyes red and blinking, body swaying.

'Now what's this all about?' he said. 'Who are you and what the hell do you want?'

Angel stared at him.

Potter wasn't much to look at but Angel supposed that on a dark night with the wind in his favour, Potter could have been the man a lonely Selina Line might have taken in matrimony, blithely unaware of all the subsequent and horrific consequences.

'I'm from the council,' Angel said. 'It's about your tickets. Are you married, Mr Potter? You could be eligible for more.'

'Course not. Don't believe in it,' he said with a loud, long laugh that showed a mouthful of big, uneven teeth. 'Bringing my children up to believe in the same,' he added. He enjoyed the hilarity so much he had to grab the door lintel to steady himself.

'And are you in full-time employment?'

'Course not,' he repeated, even louder and with a big guffaw said, 'Don't believe in it. Bringing my children up to believe in the same.' He repeated the raucous laugh and the exhibition of the teeth.

Angel tried to join in the hilarity. It wasn't easy to fake but he managed to turn up the corners of his mouth.

Potter suddenly stopped laughing and said, 'Well, what about these tickets? Lottery tickets, did you say? How many do I get?'

Angel had to think quickly. 'You're not married? Do you live here on your own?'

'What's that got to do with it?'

'To be eligible you have to have a wife or partner…one dependant at least.'

Potter screwed up his eyes as his alcohol-sodden brain began to work on the logic. A few moments later, he staggered close up to Angel's face. 'You're wasting my frigging time,' he said. 'Frig off,' he added and closed the door with a bang.

Angel turned away.

CHAPTER SEVEN

As Angel walked up the corridor and passed the CID office, Crisp saw him through the windows and rushed out into the corridor.

'I've been to the registrar's office, sir. There were eight weddings on 9 August. None of them was between a Selina Line and a Harry X.'

'How many Harrys were there?'

'None, sir. Nor Selinas. And the ages weren't any couples with similar ages. They were either much younger or much older.'

They arrived at Angel's office.

'Sit down,' he said, and Crisp took the chair by the desk.

Angel stabbed the umbrella in the sand in the fire bucket to drain and then walked the length of the room and back. He ran his hand through his hair. 'The marriage has got to be recorded there. Selina Line told her sister that she got married on Saturday 9 August. I wouldn't expect Selina to have lied about it. She'd be pleased. Delighted. Ecstatic. Presumably. Her sister, Mrs Henderson, wouldn't have got it wrong. And Harry X would have needed to marry her to smooth the way to the business of taking her purse, her jewellery and emptying her building society and bank accounts.'

Crisp shook his head. 'Nevertheless, Selina Line wasn't married in Bromersley on Saturday 9 August, sir.'

Angel stopped walking up and down and sat down at the desk. He opened his wallet and took out a postcard-size photograph and dropped it on the desk in front of Crisp. 'That's Selina Line. Get a few copies of it made and give me that one back. It belongs to Mrs Henderson. She said that this is the latest photograph she's got. Then show it to the people who conducted the marriages and see if she was a bride at any of them.'

Crisp picked up the photograph, looked at it and wrinkled his nose.

'And don't take all day,' Angel said. 'I've got another job, which might even be more urgent than that.'

Crisp looked up.

'It is still to do with this case,' Angel said, rubbing his chin. 'I have two suspects... Admittedly they are two long shots...'

He went on to tell him about the two men suspected because of their proximity to the phone box from which Selina Line had phoned her sister. He told him about both interviews in detail and described exhaustively the appearance of the red-haired young woman.

'She is obviously a tart. I want you to find her for me.'

'How can I do that, sir?'

Angel's jaw tightened. 'You're the detective. What do you think? How would *you* locate a girl on the game?'

'Go down to Canal Road after dark?'

'As a last resort, if all else fails, yes,' he snapped. 'But I expect you to use your initiative. You could start by trying to contact the Merlin Vacuum Cleaner company. See if she works for them. Frankly I don't think they exist. I suspect it's just a front, to maintain the client's respectability. You could check the PNC. She might have been through our hands or some other force's hands. In her case, she looks as if she's a cut above working in the back of cars and shop doorways. You could look in the papers. See if there are any doubtful ads. Her red hair should make her easy to find. Do you want me to do the job for you?'

'No, sir. If I can locate her, what do you want me to do?'

'Set up a meeting between us. But don't let her get a whiff that we have an interest in Laurence Potter.'

'What, sir, just between the three of us?'

Angel clenched his fists. 'No,' he bawled. '*Between her and me.*'

Crisp blinked.

'Not a single "Harry", sir. I've been through a hundred and forty-two teachers including headteachers. That's all the teachers in the borough. From kindergarten through to colleges.'

Angel frowned. 'Any Harolds?'

'No Harolds, sir,' Gawber said. 'If I had been looking for Pauls or Cliffs or Barrys, there would have been suspects for us to chase.'

'This is all very odd, Ron. Crisp has just reported in. He can find no record of the wedding of any couples that could be Selina Line and Harry X anywhere.'

Gawber frowned. 'Maybe they didn't get married?'

'Maybe they didn't. Everything that sister of hers has told us has led us nowhere.'

'Did you try the probation office, sir?'

'Yes. My friend Marie came up with two possibilities, solely because of their proximity to the telephone box; for no other reason. One of them is Dennis Schuster at 11 Edward Street. Will you see what you can find out about him and his wife Gloria surreptitiously? I don't want him knowing that we are investigating him.'

'Right, sir,' Gawber said and he went out.

Angel rubbed his chin. He was not satisfied with the information Selina Line's sister had given him. There was so little of it. What there was needed to be absolutely accurate.

He reached out for the phone. He managed to reach Josephine Henderson at The Feathers at the third attempt.

'I am so sorry I was out, Inspector. I have just returned from some shopping. What is it? Have you news of Selina?'

'I am afraid not, Mrs Henderson. We are reaching nothing but dead ends. I need to go over that conversation you had with your sister on the phone on 1 August.'

'Oh yes, well, anything, Inspector. Anything that I can do to help. That was the only time I spoke to her, after she left.'

'Yes, I understand that. She did ring later but you didn't get to the phone in time. Isn't that right?'

'Quite right.'

'Didn't she tell you she was getting married on the first call? Tell me again, please, exactly what she said, as near as you can.'

'She said that she had met a schoolteacher called Harry, that he was a widower, that they were madly in love, that he definitely wasn't married, and that they were getting married a week on Saturday. I think that was all.'

Angel frowned. 'Are you sure, Mrs Henderson? Are you absolutely certain?'

'The line wasn't very clear, Inspector. And it was rushed. And, of course, dear Selina didn't want me to know too much for fear I might have arrived and interfered with her plans. Oh dear. I do so wish that I had.'

'You mean that she may have deliberately given you false information?'

'I doubt that. She said little enough. I had no idea what part of the country she was in until I was able to have the number traced.'

'But are you sure the name of the man she gave you was Harry? We have been unable to find a single schoolteacher called Harry in the whole of the borough. Also, there is no record of a wedding service, conducted by a priest, a minister or by anybody else on 9 August of anybody called Selina or Harry.'

'Oh dear. Oh dear. I am certain that she would not have settled for anything less than a proper marriage before cohabiting with a man. She was very correct about that.'

'Would the ceremony have to have been religious, do you know?'

'A Christian church service would have been her first choice, but I can't be certain about that, Inspector.'

There was a pause.

'If there is anything I can do, Inspector...?'

'No. No. Thank you very much, Mrs Henderson. It's a puzzle, I don't mind telling you.'

'I do hope you will find her soon.'

'Oh, we will,' he said. 'I'm sure that we will,' he added.

He had said that to comfort her. He had not said that he was optimistic at finding her alive.

'Goodbye, Inspector.'

There was a knock at the door.

'Come in.'

It was DC Scrivens. 'Letter marked *Urgent* for you, sir. Just come in.'

Angel could see it was a medium large brown envelope from the British United Insurance Company, Piccadilly, London.

He took it from him. It felt soggy and the address was smudged. 'At this time? And it's wet through. Look at it.'

'It's still raining cats and dogs, sir. Reports of floods on the news. Big floods in Doncaster again. And York.'

'Right,' he said, wrinkling his nose. He stuck a letter opener into the envelope.

Scrivens went out.

Angel slit open the end and reached inside. It had three colour photographs of jewellery. There was a letter with it explaining that the photographs were sent at the request of Mrs Henderson, who had reported them missing, presumed stolen, and that the items were insured with them on an all-risk policy for a total value of £80,000, and that if they were recovered and returned to their office before 31 August, a finder's fee of ten per cent of the value would be paid out. The photographs showed a large pair of garnet earrings. The caption said that they were originally owned by a Lady Cranberry. Also a diamond and emerald necklace and an eight-carat solitaire diamond ring. He turned over each picture and on the reverse was a detailed description of the item, giving the carat weight of all the major stones. In the quietness of the office, he spent several moments admiring their beauty and memorizing them in case he should ever come across them.

Then he heard the church clock chime five o'clock.

He nodded as he heard the last dong. He was ready for home. It had been a long and tedious day. There was nothing he couldn't safely leave until tomorrow. He pushed the photographs and letter back in the envelope, squared up the pile of letters and reports not yet dealt with and put them in the top drawer. He went out of the office and as he walked down the corridor he began to consider the lack of progress he had made that day finding the missing woman. His face displayed his dissatisfaction. As he passed an outside window, he heard a clatter on the glass and glanced out; heavy rain was still beating down under pressure from squally winds. He remembered the floods of last year, both locally and in Tewkesbury, and he hoped they would not be repeated. Realizing that he'd left his umbrella behind, he turned up his jacket collar and made a dash for the car. He started the engine, put the screen wipers on fast and pulled out of the yard. He lived on a modern estate on the edge of town. Despite the rain, he made good time on the ring road, even though it was an inch deep in standing water and rain was splashing back up from the road four or five inches high. He turned off the A628 to Woodhead on to a country lane and travelled the quarter of a mile towards a Y junction. Through the wipers, he saw a yellow and black AA diversion sign blocking the road left, and a man in a yellow and black AA waterproof hat and a cape under the deluge. He signalled Angel to stop.

Angel applied the brakes, and frowned. He wondered if there had been any flooding on the estate, or if the heavy rain had caused a local landslip that had blocked the road. He remembered that there had been a landslip on the Snake

Pass last January, which had closed it to traffic. He had heard nothing and Mary would surely have phoned. He licked his lips as he considered the possibilities.

The uniformed man came up to the car and gave a salute. Angel lowered the window and as the man leaned into the car, a stream of accumulated water drained off his cape and dribbled noisily on to the ground. He noted that the poor man was soaked. He had a wide leather black strap across his chin and mouth and his hat was well pulled down so that only his eyes were visible.

'Inspector Angel?' the man said.

'Yes,' he said.

Angel had noticed, surprisingly, the distinctive smell of brandy, then, in his head, a ball rolled along a track, dropped into a hole and a bell rang.

This man was a fraud. The AA do not engage in traffic control. They haven't the authority.

Why didn't he think of it before? He was about to challenge him when the man produced a small gun from under the cape and pointed it at him.

Angel's stomach turned over. His heart thumped. His pulse raced.

'What is this?' he said, his eyes on the shiny blue Beretta.

'Shut up and do as you're told,' the man said.

His rear door was opened. At the same time, the nearside door was opened and a man got in beside him.

'Put your hands up. Look ahead,' a voice said.

Angel didn't dare move.

In the driving mirror he saw huge headlamps and a big silver radiator grille. The car behind must have been waiting, hiding in one of the farm lane ends he had passed.

The BMW rocked as a second man entered in the back. Doors slammed. He felt a jab of cold metal in the back of the neck.

A voice from the back seat from a man who sounded like he gargled in petrol said: 'Right, Mossy. Clear up here and bring the car to where we arranged.'

The man addressed as Mossy put the gun back in his pocket under the cape and dashed away.

The croaky voice from the back seat said: 'Mr Angel, shut that window and turn the car round.'

Angel recognized the accent. It was certainly from Lancashire and possibly Manchester. He glanced to his left. The man there was also holding a gun, pointing at him. He couldn't see the make. The man looked at him. It was Lloyd Corbett. *Lloyd Sexton Corbett.* It dawned on him. He was in the hands of the Corbett brothers! The Manchester killers. Wanted by three police forces at least, for murder and mayhem.

He couldn't think. He couldn't move. His breathing was irregular and his hands were unsteady. He took some small comfort in that if they had wanted him dead they would have shot him before now.

The voice more urgently said: 'Shut that window, Mr Angel, and turn the car round.'

He glanced at the windscreen. It was all steamed up. He switched on the screen blower.

There was a quick rustle of clothes behind him.

'Don't make sudden moves like that, Mr Angel,' the voice said. 'Do everything very slowly. Be careful what you do with your hands. Or I might get nervous with mine.'

Angel sat motionless in the driving seat, his face burning like a furnace. He wasn't stupid enough to rush into a situation that was more dangerous than the one he was already in, if he could possibly avoid it.

'What do you want?' Angel said.

'Just to talk, Mr Angel. Just to talk. I'm James Corbett.'

The little man on the front seat said quickly: 'And I'm Lloyd Corbett. We've already met. And I tell you, Angel, I am not in agreement with him on this. For my money, I'd sooner see you in —'

'Shut your mouth, Lloyd,' James Corbett said. 'Before I put my fist in it.' Then he jabbed Angel in the neck and said, 'Will you turn the car round, Mr Angel, and we'll go somewhere where we can talk?'

‘I talk much better when I haven’t got two guns pointing at me.’

‘I don’t take any chances, as you will come to learn. Now turn the car round, if you please.’

Angel had no choice. He put the car in gear.

James Corbett directed him back on to the A628 towards Woodhead. The road was not busy. The BMW climbed up two or three hundred feet. The landscape was grass, moss, heather and rocks. After only a short distance, they arrived at a junction and a small public house, back off the road, with a sign: *The Log Cabin. Fully licensed. Meals available.*

Angel reckoned it needed a coat of paint. Two coats. It looked a deadbeat place in the rain. He was told to turn right on to the large empty gravel car park at the side and stop as near the front entrance as possible.

James Corbett said: ‘Switch off the engine. Give me the keys.’

Angel turned round to face him. He looked into his small black eyes, like bilberries in milk. It was hate at first sight. James Corbett took the keys. He smiled with his mouth but not with his eyes.

Lloyd Corbett got out of the car first. ‘Come on,’ he said, standing in the heavy rain. ‘Quick. Let’s get inside.’ He was still holding a gun and pointing it at Angel. ‘Get out,’ he said.

James Corbett got out of the back and pointed his gun at Angel and said: ‘Inside. Quick. Let’s go.’

Angel got out. He glanced round as he kicked his way through the occasional thistle and tuft of grass sprouting through the gravel.

Lloyd Corbett led the way, and the three men ran up two steps, through the door into the deserted bar.

Lloyd pushed his way through the empty tables, chairs and gaming machines to a door at the end. It opened into a small room. Angel followed him inside. There were six small tables, around twenty-four chairs, a big window overlooking the road and the magnificent heather-covered mountain beyond, and that was all. The sort of room that may have been used for after-hours drinking or private card schools.

James Corbett said: 'Turn round, Mr Angel. Put your hands on the wall.' He turned to Lloyd and said: 'All right, Lloyd. Make a good job of it.'

Lloyd Corbett glared back at him with wild eyes. 'I *always* make a good job of it.'

The little man stuffed the gun in his pocket and patted Angel down from neck to ankle, along his arms and all the way down his legs.

Angel had to hand it to him, he was as thorough as a Spaniel looking for amphetamines in a cargo of onions.

When he was satisfied, he turned to his brother and nodded.

'Sit down, Mr Angel,' James Corbett said, pulling out a chair.

Angel deliberately chose a chair from a different table and sat down. His trouser legs slapped coldly against his knees and shins. It was then that he realized how wet he was. He wiped his face with his handkerchief.

James Corbett pulled a face. 'Now let's all try and be reasonable.'

'I'm always reasonable,' Lloyd Corbett said. 'This is a load of crap.'

James Corbett's jaw stiffened. He raised his shoulders and towered over the little man. 'You're the crap, Lloyd. You always have been. Now shut your mouth and get out of here. I don't know why I put up with you. Get out. Get out and stay out.'

He bustled him towards the door.

Lloyd's face was scarlet. 'I'm going. I'm going. I still say it's a crap idea.'

James Corbett slammed the door behind him. Then he immediately reopened it and said, 'Fetch some drinks. Make yourself useful.'

He turned back to Angel.

'Sit down,' he said. 'Sit down. Excuse him. He has no brains. He's the runt of the litter. Take no notice of him. I run this show. I only keep him on out of charity. Family. You understand?'

Angel didn't respond. He wasn't sure what would be safe to say.

'Relax, Mr Angel. You will be wondering why I invited you to have this little chat with me.'

Angel rubbed his chin and nodded. 'Unusual sort of invitation,' he said.

The corners of Corbett's mouth turned up and a few teeth were flashed.

Angel thought it was a smile, although he had once seen a snake smile more convincingly.

The door opened noisily and Lloyd Corbett came in carrying a black tin tray with two half-full tumblers of a brown liquid on it. He took the tray over to James Corbett and put one of the glasses on the table in front of him.

'Brandy,' he said.

James Corbett didn't seem to notice. He maintained an interested gaze on Angel.

Lloyd Corbett came over to Angel and banged the other glass in front of him, causing it to splash on the table top.

Angel noticed but he had no intention of drinking it.

Lloyd then looked at his brother with raised eyebrows. James replied with a gesture with his thumb to go away. Lloyd jeered, waved, went out and slammed the door.

James Corbett picked up the tumbler and took a drink. As he swallowed, he looked at the tumbler agreeably and then put it down on the table.

Angel's stomach had almost settled, his breathing much more even, but the muscles round his jaw were still taut. 'What do you want with me?' he said.

'The question could be the other way round,' James Corbett said. 'You have been looking for me and Lloyd. Our pictures are all over town, with your name at the bottom.

Says you want to know where we are. Well, we're here. Now what?'

'Simple,' Angel said. 'I want you to get out of Bromersley.'

Corbett beamed. 'That's not very friendly.'

Angel didn't reply.

Corbett's face hardened. 'I've met coppers like you before. You put on a very hard front. It jacks up the price. All right. You can play around a bit. I don't mind. Business is good. I can afford it. You've got good negotiating skills, Angel. I'll give you that.'

Angel could sense a bribe coming on. 'I can't be bought off, Corbett,' he said. 'All I want you to do is go back from where you came.'

The snake's smile grew wider. 'Oh, you *are* good. You should be on the telly.'

'You don't want to be hanging around Bromersley, Corbett. Don't you realize that when Charlie Drumme gets out of hospital, he'll come looking for you?'

His eyebrows shot up. 'Don't know what you're talking about. Never heard of him.'

'You, or your lieutenants, put Charlie Drumme in hospital because you want to take over his turf.'

'I told you, I never heard of him.'

'He runs a string of girls down the Canal Road, and he has a small grass business in some of the small ailing pubs around the town. If the law was tighter and there were more hours in the day, we would have had the street cleared, his factory closed down and he'd be inside doing time. I would have thought that taking over his business would have been small beer to a big noise like you.'

'Look, Angel,' he said. 'Let's stop dancing round the outside. I can't discuss my plans with you until I know you're on board. I've got fantastic plans. Plans you wouldn't believe. I'm talking millions. You can be part of those plans. I've got control of a big piece of Lancashire and I am ready to expand. You don't *have* to be a grubby little copper for the rest of your life.'

Angel smiled wryly and rubbed a hand across his mouth. 'You've a chief constable and a superintendent senior to me,' he said. 'And two other inspectors at my rank. You're going to need a simply huge bag of goodies to get you a police-free passage through Bromersley.'

'Yeah, but I needn't bother about the others, need I? If I've got you on my team, we can work round them, can't we? You're the brains of the outfit. You're top banana, aren't you?'

'It doesn't work like that, Corbett. And I'm not top banana, as you put it.'

He smiled. 'I like that. I like a modest man. If there's one thing I like it's a modest man. I'm a modest man myself.'

'Yes, well, from what I've heard,' Angel said, 'you've a lot to be modest about.'

The smile vanished from Corbett's face.

Angel regretted the easy insult. It had not been necessary. No, he reflected, but it had been fun.

Corbett's face went red. 'Let's stop frigging around,' he shouted. 'What I want from you is a deal…cooperation.'

'Such as shutting a blind eye to yesterday's Pelican Security van robbery?'

Corbett was momentarily stunned. Under half-closed eyelids, his pupils slid to the left, to the right and then back again.

Angel had hit home. It had only been a stab in the dark. He must be careful though. He had to get out of this situation in one piece. 'I couldn't do anything about that even if I wanted to,' he added. 'It isn't my case.'

Corbett's fists tightened. He shook his head impatiently. 'Never mind that,' he bawled. 'I mean a long-term, wide-ranging arrangement. I'm talking really big money.'

Angel's attention was suddenly taken by some activity through the big window. A big antique Rolls-Royce had pulled off the carriageway on to the gravel car park. It had huge silver headlamps and a shiny silver radiator grille. It would be the car he saw in his reversing mirror standing behind him when he had first been stopped. The driver parked it next to the BMW. The driver was the one who had been in the AA man's uniform, the one Corbett had called Mossy. Angel noticed that it was still raining hard, as rain was still bouncing off the car's polished black roof.

When Corbett saw the car's arrival, his face brightened. He jumped up from the table, dashed across to the door, yanked it open and called, 'Lloyd! Lloyd! Fetch me that box from the car.'

He heard a disgruntled reply.

Then James Corbett came back into the room.

A minute or two later, Lloyd Corbett came in with a small cardboard box. His face was like thunder. He totally ignored Angel. He shoved the box roughly into James Corbett's hand and said: 'This is frigging ridiculous. I have told you.'

'Shut up and get out,' James Corbett said.

Lloyd Corbett shook his head and said: 'I'm going. I'm going, but don't say I didn't tell you.' He went out and closed the door.

James Corbett switched on the smile. He walked over to where Angel was sitting, and put the small box on the table in front of him. 'That's the first payment of £20,000 in used notes and different denominations. If all goes well, as I expect it to do, and you cooperate in my plans, I should be able to pay you that sum every month. In a year that would amount to £240,000. In four years you'd be a millionaire.'

Angel looked at the box and sighed. He didn't expect the bribe to be as much as £20,000. It must be inflation. His heart sank. His situation was unenviable. He had to decline this obnoxious offer without rousing Corbett's anger. He stroked his chin. He wanted to get out of this position alive.

Corbett stared down at him. 'Well, what do you say?'

Angel couldn't think of anything smart to say. 'No,' he said. 'No. It's not my style. I don't do bribes.'

Corbett frowned, pursed his lips, turned round and walked away. After a few moments he came back. The smile was even bigger. He nodded and said, 'I know you, Michael Angel. I heard you had a devious mind, and that you could out-think anybody you came up against. All right. All right. But I don't know how you do it. I don't know how you could possibly know that *that* was not my best offer?'

Angel brushed his hand through his hair. The situation was impossible.

'It's not that,' Angel said as earnestly as he could. 'It's simple. I don't take bribes. Contrary to popular belief, policemen don't take bribes.'

'I understand,' Corbett said with a smile. The deal is, of course, £25,000 a month. I have another £5,000 in the car. How you knew, I cannot understand. Nowhere in the world has a copper ever had such an offer.'

He looked down at Angel.

Angel shook his head. But he understood how policemen (and others) could be so easily led into such trouble. He sometimes found it difficult to find money at the end of the month. He still owed several thousand on their mortgage, and he was a week or two behind with the gas bill. £25,000 would clear it all off beautifully. To be free of debt and have a few thousand in the bank would be magic. But he knew it could not possibly happen.

'I don't take bribes, Corbett. I don't take bribes. Don't you understand?'

There was the tinkle of a mobile phone.

Angel knew it wasn't his.

Corbett dived into his pocket, pulled out a phone and looked at the LCD. His face creased up and he bared his teeth. He pressed a button on the phone, put it to his mouth and screamed: '*What is it, Laura? I'm very busy*. I told you not to ring me unless it was important.'

Angel couldn't hear Laura's side of the conversation, but she was loud, expressive and she spoke continuously for about a minute.

'All right,' Corbett said at length. He sighed. 'All right. Yes. *I'm coming now*.'

He closed the phone and pushed it into his pocket. He walked towards the door and then back again. He looked at Angel and made one more circuit. When he returned he said, 'I know what it is, Michael, you want time to think about it.'

'No, I don't,' Angel said.

He simply wanted to reject the deal. He didn't want to antagonize the man. He wanted to walk out of the place alive and go home to his wife Mary, that's all. What more could he say?

Corbett didn't want to hear that.

'I'll be in touch,' he said, and he walked out of the room. Angel wondered if he was leaving. It would mean he was free. He jumped to his feet, ready for a quick exit.

He heard men shouting in the bar, then footsteps rapidly coming back towards him. He sat down. What were they coming back for?

Lloyd Corbett came into the room. He dashed over to where Angel was seated and grabbed the cardboard box from the table. He turned, hesitated at the door and said, 'Here, Angel. Have you come across The Fixer on your travels?'

Angel frowned. 'No.'

He pulled an ugly face. 'If you do — a tip for you — kill him before he kills you,' he said and rushed off.

Angel blinked in amazement, and wondered what Lloyd Corbett meant by it.

Seconds later, through the window, he saw the Corbetts pile into the back of the Rolls-Royce and saw it pull away rapidly from the front of The Log Cabin. It turned left towards Bromersley.

He let out a long sigh. He was alive. He was free. He couldn't believe it. He dashed out of the room into the empty bar/dining area to make for the door. Then he remembered, his car keys were in James Corbett's pocket.

He heard a voice behind him call out. 'Is your name Mr Angel?'

He frowned, turned and saw a little man in a white hat dodging round at the back of a coffee machine behind the serving counter.

'Yes,' he said.

The man dangled a set of car keys at the end of his fingers. 'I was told to give you these.'

Angel smiled. His car keys. That was fantastic. If he put his foot down, it was possible to catch up with them, follow them and find out where they were hiding out.

He dashed up to the counter, his hand outstretched.

'There's a message goes with them,' the man said, smiling.

'Oh yes?'

'They said to tell you that they noticed you had two flat tyres.'

CHAPTER FOUR

It was 0828 hours the following morning, Friday 22 August.

At last the rain had stopped and the sky was a clear blue.

The headline news on the radio and television was still about people flooded out of their houses, broken river-banks, roads swamped, clogged sewers and trains delayed. The weathermen were pointing out that while locations above sea level would soon dry out after the heavy drenching, water would still be soaking down from the hill and mountain tops for the next few days, adding to the existing troubles in low-lying and vulnerable places.

Angel was in his office, on the phone speaking to DS Donald Taylor, head of SOCO.

'It was an old Rolls-Royce, Don,' Angel said. 'Probably 1920s or 30s. The number plates were false but that was to be expected. I want you to see if you can recover any tyre tracks. The tyres were very wide, it won't be difficult to spot which vehicle it is. But you'll have to move fast, before the tracks are all driven over.'

'Right, sir.'

'I've sent Ed Scrivens along to your office with the addresses of the sites and my sketches and notes of the likely places where you might be able to find them. He should be with you any second.'

'We'll move as soon as he gets here, sir.'

He replaced the phone but it rang immediately. He lifted the receiver. It was DS Crisp. 'Yes?'

'I've been round the eight people who actually married a couple on 9 August, sir,' he said. 'They each only performed the one ceremony that day, and none of them recognized Selina Line. In fact, they all say they don't ever recall having seen her.'

Angel sighed.

'I have been thinking, sir,' Crisp said. 'Either the photograph's wrong, or she simply didn't get married on the ninth. I mean, the root source of this information was the registrar. She can't be wrong, can she?'

'No. And the supporting information I have is directly from her sister and she should know. Now, I want to make this particular line of inquiry a hundred per cent conclusive. Go back to the registrar and get a comprehensive list of priests, ministers and whatever who are authorized to marry people in Bromersley. You'll have to be nice to her. Then visit each one, show him or her the photograph of Selina Line and find out if they've married her in the past, say, three weeks. All right?'

'Yes. Right, sir. I might have some difficulty getting to the little churches out in the wilds, like Hoylandswaine, Tunistone and Slogmarrow. Did you know Creesforth Dam Road is closed to traffic? The dam was in danger of flooding. The sluice gate is reputed to be cluttered up with rubbish.'

'Is it? You can go round the bottom road.'

'No, sir. That's flooded. And Bromersley Bottom might be flooded if the dam doesn't hold. They say that it is at a dangerous level.'

'Really?'

'There's a crane working from the road to clear rubbish from the sluice gates...so that the overflow dam water can get away more quickly. It was on the news.'

'I hadn't heard. Well, you'll have to do the best you can. Get round there when the road is reopened. Thank goodness the rain has stopped. Have you made any progress on the other matter? Finding the woman with red hair?'

'Not much, sir. I haven't had the time.'

'I'm not chasing you. Just anxious.'

'I have found out one thing, sir,' he said. 'That there's no such company as Merlin Vacuum Cleaners.'

Angel smiled. He wasn't surprised.

It was an old ruse for 'working girls' to pretend to be selling vacuum cleaners or some other domestic appliance on their visits to houses, particularly helpful to them in areas where their clients had nosy neighbours.

'All right, lad. Get on with it and keep in touch.'

He replaced the phone, eased himself back in the swivel chair and rubbed his chin. He wondered why he was having so much difficulty finding Selina Line. The wedding was proving difficult to trace, and it shouldn't be. He ran his hand through his hair. He only had Josephine Henderson's word that Selina Line had phoned from the phone box on Victoria Road on 1 August and told her that she was getting married on the ninth. It made him think. If the phone company had said that the call had come from Berlin, then presumably she would have flown there and had the German police scratching round the churches, chapels, town halls and wherever else it was now legal for two people to be married.

He sighed noisily. Nevertheless, he didn't believe that Mrs Henderson had an ulterior motive. If she had, why would she have picked on Bromersley? It would have been far easier and more convenient for her to have selected somewhere nearer home in Surrey.

He knew that he wouldn't be able to check on Selina's phone call to Mrs Henderson with the phone company, as too much time had elapsed. He would simply have to believe her. It was just that it seemed impossible to find any trace of Selina Line anywhere. All inquiries so far had drawn a blank.

It was as if she didn't exist. He suddenly had a thought. He leaned forward to lower his chair, opened the middle desk drawer and took out one of the photographs of the missing woman that he had had printed. Then he looked in his address book, picked up the phone and tapped out a number.

He spoke to the assistant editor of the *Bromersley Chronicle*, the local weekly rag, and made an arrangement to reproduce the photograph with the headline, 'Have you seen this woman?' It would be presented in next Friday's issue on the front page with a paragraph of description and so on.

He replaced the phone, sighed and nodded. That was the first stage of going public with the inquiry. His heart somehow felt lighter.

He reflected over the conversations he had had with Josephine Henderson again and the more he thought about it, he felt instinctively that she was telling the truth. The entire inquiry hinged on that. She had better be.

There was a knock at the door. It was Gawber.

'Come in, Ron. Sit down. What have you got?'

'About Dennis Schuster and his missus?'

'Yes. Yes,' Angel said enthusiastically.

'Well, I discovered that he isn't a contributor to the Inland Revenue, for a start.'

'That's no surprise.'

'And according to the Benefits Agency in Newcastle, he's been claiming unemployed benefit since 2000. But before that I did find a link previously to teaching.'

Angel looked up.

'He was employed as a peripatetic musician, teaching piano in various schools in the borough until 2000. I don't suppose any school would touch him when they discovered he had a criminal record.'

Angel rubbed his chin. 'Crooks and kids don't mix,' he said. 'But then we're not expecting our villain to tell the truth, are we? Villains like to say something near the truth, and to a conman like Schuster, it must have seemed quite respectable for him to tell his exceedingly rich bride-to-be that he was a schoolteacher, don't you think? Education is still a very respectable profession.'

'I agree, sir.'

'But Schuster would need a house, a place of some sort, to take Selina for two or three weeks. That terraced house on Edward Street hardly seems imposing enough. Did you check with the council? Does he pay rates or rent on any other property?'

Gawber smiled wryly. 'He was behind with his council tax. He was two years behind with the council rates on 11 Edward Street, until last week he paid the bill in full, over a thousand pounds. Looks like he suddenly came into money.'

Angel frowned. 'That man is beginning to look interesting.'

'Is there enough for us to get a search warrant, sir?'

'I really don't think so. We need proof that Selina is missing, some indication that she actually arrived in Bromersley and then that somebody murdered her. We don't know any of those things for a fact yet. What we've got is only circumstantial.'

Gawber's jaw dropped. It was true. All these inquiries stemmed from what must have been a convincing scenario put before Angel by Mrs Henderson. It seemed to him that his boss was on quite a risky mission.

'We need more. If we can get him on any other crime, we could maybe get a search warrant and get round it that way.'

Gawber nodded.

'There's obviously money tumbling into that house from somewhere. He's not working, so where's the money coming from? Is his wife working?'

'No. Checked on that.'

'Right. I want you to shadow him for a couple of days. Take a camera. I can't offer you a mate. Just sit out there and find out who comes and who goes, and where he goes and what he does.'

'It's Friday, sir. When do you want me to start?'

'Are you looking for any overtime?'

'Not now the weather's turned nice.'

'Do it today and Monday then. Let's hope we're lucky.'

'Right, sir.'

Angel's eyes followed him out. He watched the door close. Then he turned to the pile of post and reports on his desk. He fingered through the envelopes and was about to open one when the phone rang. It was the superintendent. He could tell by the wheezy intake of breath before he spoke.

'Come up here, lad. Smartly.'

'Right, sir,' Angel said. He pulled a face. A visit to Harker's office was rarely a pleasant experience. He trudged up the green corridor, wondering what had prodded him into life that Friday morning. It couldn't be the matter of the missing Nigel Monro and the ruby egg. Angel had not pursued that since Harker had ordered him to drop it. It seemed that that case would have to be investigated in his own time. He had given his word to Sir Max that he would see that the ruby was delivered to the Princess Yasmin. It might not be possible, seeing as how the ruby wasn't in the safe as it should have been, but he must do what he can. He may have to find the whereabouts of Nigel Monro first in order to be able to recover the ruby.

He arrived at the superintendent's office, knocked on the door and went in.

Harker began speaking as soon as the door was closed. 'I see from a report from one of your sergeants that he's been making trips to priests, ministers and wedding clerks. What's that all about?'

Angel looked up. 'It's a case that came to me direct, sir. A woman, a very rich woman, name of Selina Line, has gone missing, and her sister is particularly concerned for her safety. Selina Line ran away from home and took up a relationship with a man in Bromersley. She apparently married him on 9 August. I have been trying to establish the details of the marriage so that we can identify the man and interview him. Up to date, I have had no success. The missing woman managed to keep the wedding a mysterious secret.'

Harker rose, his nose turned up and the corners of his mouth turned down. He sniffed then said: 'Sounds like a tale from a schoolgirls' Penny Dreadful.'

'The sister is very worried, sir,' Angel said. 'The woman withdrew all her money from her bank and building society accounts, took with her jewellery worth £80,000 and nothing has been heard of her since. She suspects that her sister's been abducted.'

'Local family?'

'No, sir. They're from Surrey.'

His ginger eyebrows shot up. 'Surrey? *Surrey*? What are we doing helping Surrey with *their* crime figures? They've never done anything for us. And, anyway, what is the connection of the missing woman with Bromersley?'

'The missing woman's sister in Surrey traced a phone call she had had from her to the phone box on Victoria Road.'

'Is that all? Nothing else?'

'No, sir.'

'Don't you realize, one digit wrong and the call could have come from...from anywhere. I think you've gone round the twist, lad. This is obviously a case for missing persons. Send the sister to the Salvation Army. They do mispers better than anybody. Even if the phone box is the right one, maybe the woman *wanted* to be carried off to a love nest with a bit of Yorkshire rough. What's it got to do with you?'

'It doesn't sound right. She is middle-aged, not used to socializing. Lived under the shadow of her father. Her father died, left her a fortune.'

'Have you any proof that the woman is in danger?'

'No, sir. I don't suppose —'

'Well, until that happens, forget it. Our hands are tied.'

'It doesn't...smell right, sir.'

'Forget it. We can't afford to finance an inquiry that should be undertaken by another force. What do you think this is, lad, a charity?'

'It *is* a public service, sir.'

'One woman isn't the public, lad. What is it with you? Ever since you gained a certain attention in the media for solving murder cases, you think that this station revolves round you. I think that *you* think it's your own personal support centre. Well, it isn't. You've got to mesh in with everybody else. Work as part of a team. Work in a disciplined way. This case is clearly a missing person case. It is not for us to be involved unless a crime has been committed. You know that damned well. What is it, lad? Is the woman who reported it a good-looker or something? Have you started fancying a bit on the side? It happens to middle-aged men. You'd not be the first copper to lose his marbles at the hand of a sweet-talking bird, with a big bank balance and a good pair of legs.'

Angel's heart was thumping. His lips tightened against his teeth. 'No, sir,' he said. 'The lady is charming enough, but that's nothing to do with it. My marbles are in perfect order. It is that there are other factors in this case that justify me continuing with it.'

'But we don't *want* to continue with it,' bawled Harker. 'You're still trying to find reasons why we *should* continue with it, I'm trying to find reasons to get out of it. This is a misper case, the woman should be directed to the Salvation Army. If there is more to it, it should be passed on to the Surrey force where it rightfully belongs. Let them do it. Their budget will be ten times ours.'

'There's more crime down there.'

'*That's why their budget is ten times ours*. It isn't as if her body has been found in the borough. She's probably whooping it up with her Casanova in some five-star hotel on the French Riviera. Now I don't want to hear any more about it.'

Angel's face dropped. His thought processes were being thrown into disarray. He would have to review the situation and make some compromise plan. He certainly had no intention of abandoning the case: he had committed far too much personal emotional energy and time into it. He couldn't leave the matter unresolved.

'Now what I really want to know,' Harker said, 'is how you are getting along with the business of the four men with the broken fingers. It's almost two months since the offence. How are you getting along with *that*?'

Angel crisply told the superintendent that PC Ahmed Ahaz was making a list of comparisons, to find matching facts of all four men that hopefully would lead to unravelling the mysterious reason for the assault.

Harker didn't seem pleased with the idea but he didn't suggest any other lines of inquiry. He simply gave him a general pep talk about sticking closely to the brief of cases only allotted to him and that was that.

Angel couldn't get out of the office fast enough. He charged down the corridor and turned into the CID room.

Ahmed was at a desk by the door. He was tapping on a computer keyboard.

'How's it going, lad?' Angel said.

The young man looked up in surprise. 'Only slow, sir. I think I have run out of questions.'

Angel shook his head. 'You can never run out of questions,' he said pursing his lips. 'Have you gone back to their schooldays? Have you asked them which schools they went to?'

'Yes, sir. There are no similarities there.'

'Hobbies? Gardens? Pets?'

'Yes, sir. Done all that.'

'It's a bit obvious, but did you ask about any rings they might have worn or even used to wear?'

'Yes, sir.'

'Wives, children, their ages. Get dates. Anything years back happened to them all on 24 June? The date they were attacked. Always get the dates of events. You might get something to match there.'

Ahmed's face brightened. 'Yes, sir.'

'Are the four men cooperating with you all right?'

'Yes, sir. They're mostly as keen as we are to get an explanation.'

'Good. Good. Keep at it. You're doing a really good job, Ahmed. I know it's boring and repetitive, but you mustn't get lost by the rhythm and repetition of the thing. Don't lose sight of what this is all about.'

'No, sir,' he said.

'We are trying to find a link, a clue, something that applies to all four men, something that is the same to each of them. Something that all these four men have, are, did, have experienced, owned or whatever, in common. And that will help us to solve the mystery.'

Ahmed sighed. 'I'll never do it.'

'Yes, you will,' Angel said. 'It's a matter of persistence. Keep at it. I'm relying on you.'

'Right, sir,' he said, and he turned back to the computer, looked up at the screen and began to tap purposefully on the keyboard.

Angel hovered for a moment and watched him. He smiled and decided that he had said enough. He went out of the room and crossed to his own office. On the desk he saw that somebody had put an email under a polythene bag containing a pair of handcuffs that he had indented for. He frowned, put the handcuffs in the drawer and picked up the email.

It read:

From Detective Superintendent Cheetham, Lamb Road Police Station, Sturdingham, Herts.

To all senior ranks, all 43 forces.

Following the shooting dead yesterday of Terence Patrick Gilfillan, 23, fairground worker, of Dublin, Liverpool and lately of Milton Keynes, who was awaiting trial for drug trafficking and selling, I am urgently needing to talk to a man known as The Fixer who was seen in the vicinity and is strongly suspected of this murder.

The Fixer is around 5' 10" tall, 160 lbs, dark navy blue suit, collar and tie. He is armed and carries a Walther PPK/S 32 automatic. He is also believed to have been responsible for the murder of Paul Muller, robber of Liverpool, last month, and several other murders in London.

I would be grateful for any information on any suspect that may pass through your hands, who you might consider to be The Fixer.

Message ends.

He sat down and read the email again, then he lowered it on to the desk. The Fixer. That was the second time that name had come up. He sounded to be a nasty piece of work. He would have to keep his eye open for him. He noted the description of the man. There wasn't much. He found it easy to memorize.

The phone rang. It was Crisp, sounding very pleased with himself. He had found the red-haired young woman Angel had spotted strutting unsteadily out of Laurence Potter's house with the empty Merlin Vacuum Cleaner box.

'Her name's Valerie, sir. She accosted me, well, sort of…'

'In daylight hours? Where?'

'Well, she used to go to The Fisherman's Rest at lunch-time, before the smoking ban. Now she doesn't do pubs, she says. I caught up with her in Mrs Chin's Little House of Happiness, up Barrel Street. Acupuncture, Chinese massage, skin treatments, specialist aromatic oils, that sort of thing. Above the Chinese takeaway. I said I wouldn't arrest her provided that she helped us with some general information.'

Angel blinked. 'I can't meet her there,' he said.

'Oh no, sir. She'd only agree to meet in a neutral place. The best place I could get her to agree to was the picnic area in Jubilee Park.'

CHAPTER NINE

Since the rain had stopped, the sky had turned bright blue and the sun had shone continuously, which made the picnic area of Jubilee Park a pleasant place to make a tryst. The area comprised twenty tables with fitted benches on two sides to seat four people to a table. The sun had thoroughly dried out the tables and seats, which were warm to the touch, but even so, only a handful of people occupied them.

Angel had already surveyed the location, been into the park café opposite and bought a small packet of digestive biscuits and some thin weak tea in a cardboard cup. He had chosen a table furthest away from two separate couples who were enjoying the sun and each other's company. He sipped the tea, then checked his watch. It was four o'clock straight up. He wrinkled his nose and wondered why women were always late.

A young woman with red hair and a short skirt was crossing from the direction of the café. She strutted across to him confidently. He recognized her and stood up.

'Valerie?'

Close up, her make-up was cracked like blistered paint and her uncovered chest was like a kitchen-sink draining board.

'You must be the copper,' she said with the look of a patient about to have a flu jab.

He nodded. 'Can I get you a tea or anything?'

She flashed him an appreciative smile. She didn't get many courtesies from attractive men those days.

'Brought my own,' she said, lifting a long, uncovered leg inside the bench to sit down.

He had to admit she had shapely legs.

'Only drink my own now,' she said, unlatching the buckle of a thick leather satchel she had been carrying on a shoulder strap. She fished inside and brought out a small glass bottle half filled with a clear liquid. She shook it at him and said meaningfully: 'I've had my drink spiked for the last time.'

Angel watched her unscrew the top and take a swig; he guessed it was white rum. As she screwed back the top, she curled her lips and shook her head as if she hadn't really enjoyed it.

'You're not going to do the dirty on me and arrest me, are you?'

'Certainly not.'

'I must be crackers. I was told it was to help a missing woman else I wouldn't be here. I'm not even certain this is a good idea. I don't suppose there's a reward or anything?'

'Only the satisfaction that you might save a woman's life.'

She smiled. 'Huh. Come off it. Don't try and appeal to my better nature because I haven't got one. If I can help you, I hope that if I ever get in trouble you'll let me off.'

'Won't be able to do that, Valerie. But if you're ever in trouble, ask for me. I'll help you if I can. All right?'

He took a business card out of his wallet and pushed it in front of her.

She looked at it and then into his eyes briefly. 'All right, Detective Inspector Angel, what exactly do you want?' she said as she put the card in a purse inside the leather bag.

'It's like this,' he said. 'I am looking for a missing woman. She'd be older than you, but not a woman of the world like you. Her mother died years ago, and she was brought up under the protection — heavy protection, I suspect — of her father, who was a successful, wealthy man. She never wanted for anything, but knows little about marriage, villains, deceit and liars. She would be used to mingling in a world of people of gentleness, honesty and wealth. Her father died two years ago. She has an older sister, who sort of stood in for her father, but she hadn't the authority, I suppose. Anyway, she inherited half her father's fortune, which was a helluva lot, and recently left the family home. Inquiries show that she arrived in Bromersley and mysteriously married somebody a fortnight ago. We have no idea who the man is. Now she has completely disappeared. Have you come across anybody like that?'

'Didn't know there *was* anybody like that. Anyway, why pick on me? Why would I know any more than a thousand others?'

'We have a shortlist of people who might have…known her.'

Valerie licked her lips for a moment. Her eyes darted here and there. 'Yeah, but I didn't.'

'Laurence Potter is a…a friend of yours.'

The pupils of her eyes jumped. 'Laurence Potter? Not a friend. A client, Inspector Angel. A client, nothing more. You don't suspect him, do you? If she had married him, where is she now? She wasn't there yesterday!'

Angel didn't answer.

Her eyes suddenly stopped moving around as she worked out answers to her own questions. She reached out for the bottle, unscrewed the cap quickly and took another swig.

'How long have you known him?'

'Yesterday was the first and only time.'

'How did you make contact?'

'He phoned me. I leave my photograph with my mobile number printed on it in pubs and clubs and…other places. He wouldn't have a problem finding a girl like me in Bromersley. There's plenty of competition. Huh.'

Angel shook his head when he heard her say 'other places'. By that, he thought she meant phone booths, which she would know was illegal. She was playing canny; she still didn't trust him.

'Was he difficult negotiating?'

'Easy as pie. I went straight round. He paid like a lamb.'

Angel nodded. 'He was pretty drunk when I was talking to him.'

'Yeah. He was drunk when I arrived and he was more drunk when I left. He was drinking champagne. We both were.'

Angel's eyes flashed. 'Champagne, eh? Was he celebrating something special?'

'I don't know,' she said. 'He didn't say, but he was… happy, yes.'

'Lives on his own, we understand.'

'Looked like it.'

'Was there any sign that a woman had been there?' he said quickly. 'Any clothes? Make-up? Any little thing? Coat behind the door? Slippers in the kitchen? Any fresh flowers in the house at all?'

'No. No. I didn't see anything like that.'

He rubbed his chin. 'Would you say he was used to… entertaining ladies?'

'You mean entertaining ladies like me. Yes. He wasn't new to the…business.' Then suddenly she changed. Her eyes looked straight ahead at nothing in particular. 'You know, it's frightening when you think about it,' she said, her fingers tightening round the bottle. 'It would have been so easy for him to have strangled me and then taken his money back.'

'But *he didn't*,' Angel said.

'Do you think he murdered her, the missing woman?'

'At this stage he is only a suspect, with many others. He fits one or two criteria, that's all.'

She shuddered. 'I'm not going back there.'

He saw her arm turn to gooseflesh and her fingers trembling.

'There. There,' Angel said. He wanted to hold her hands, but he knew he must not.

'Now I think about him, he gives me the creeps,' she said.

'You don't have to go back there. You're here now. You're safe. You've nothing to fear from him.'

Her eyes were glazed over. He wanted to shake her. 'Listen,' he said.

He waited a few moments. She stayed motionless.

'Valerie. Valerie. You're safe now. You've nothing to fear from him.'

She looked at him.

'Listen. I am looking for a man who has abducted a woman and possibly murdered her. Please try and help me. At this time, it is the best thing you can do for me as well as yourself.'

'I know. I know. And I will. Ask me anything you like.'

He licked his lips and said, 'What did he do for a living? Where did the money come from for you, for the champagne? Did he say?'

'He didn't say. But the house was well furnished and everything seemed new. A big new slimline telly, three-piece suite, new estate car at the back, and so on. The place was scruffy but there seemed to be no shortage of money.'

That bothered Angel. 'The person I am looking for said he was a widower, that his name was Harry and that he was a schoolteacher. We can't make any sense of those claims.'

She thought a moment. Hesitantly, she replied, 'He may have been a widower. I wouldn't know. I didn't know his first name. I called him Mr Potter. He may have been a schoolteacher, but I wouldn't have thought so. That's really all I know. Sorry.'

Angel looked at her, nodded and said, 'Well, thanks very much, Valerie. If you think of anything, please give me a ring.'

She smiled.

He stood up and stepped out of the bench seat.

'Just a minute,' she said as she rummaged in her shoulder bag. 'Don't rush off.' She looked up at him, smiled and handed him a photographic card with her mobile phone number on it. 'I do special rates for nice-looking coppers.'

The heavy rain having come to an end on Friday last meant that Angel had had no excuse to dodge gardening over the weekend. Following some haranguing by his wife Mary, he had cut the lawn, the hedge, deadheaded all round and hoed the borders diligently so that there was not a weed in sight. As a consequence, he was delighted to get to his desk that Monday morning even though it was August Bank Holiday and most of the force were not working.

Angel and his team from CID were working as normal. They had had Easter off, so it was only fair to his opposite number. He was hoping it would be uneventful so that he could clear some of the paperwork off his desk.

However, before he had had chance to touch it, the phone rang. It was the civilian telephonist on the switchboard to tell him that Mrs Dunleavy was on the line.

The old lady didn't sound very happy.

'Oh dear, Inspector Angel, I am so glad that you are there.'

'Nice to hear from you, Mrs Dunleavy,' he said. He didn't mean it, but the old lady was such a dear. 'What is the news? Has Nigel turned up?'

'Indeed he has not. I wondered if you had any news of him. You don't think after all this time, Inspector, that he may have...passed away?'

'I really have no idea, Mrs Dunleavy. What are you doing now? Surely you have left the Monro house and returned to your own home?'

'Indeed I have. I have locked up Sir Max's house and taken the keys to Mr Pugh — he's Mr Nigel's solicitor as well as Sir Max's, you know. I have also taken him a load of mail that has come since Sir Max died, mostly for Mr Nigel, and mostly from The Northern Bank, I might add. Mr Pugh said that I was not to worry. He explained that he believed that Nigel's trouble started when the credit squeeze began, which resulted in a run on that bank last September.'

'Yes, of course. Is Mr Pugh happy to take on sorting Nigel's matters out? It sounds such a mammoth task.'

'Well, he said he would do what he can. He really needs Mr Nigel to contact him, although I wonder if he'll get paid. Nigel owes such a lot of money.'

'Well, don't you worry about it, Mrs Dunleavy. It's not your responsibility. You have done all you can.'

'That's what Mr Pugh said. Do you think I have done the best thing, Inspector?'

'Absolutely. You should not be acting as a buffer between Nigel and his creditors. I urge you to withdraw from it, settle down and enjoy your retirement.'

'I will try to, but I can't help but worry about him, and wonder where he is now.'

'Sheltering from his creditors, I expect,' Angel said. 'Of course, I don't suppose the ruby has turned up.'

'Huh. You won't see it again, Inspector. I know where *that's* gone,' she said meaningfully.

Angel hoped she was wrong.

'There's nothing more I should do to help then, Inspector?' she said.

'Nothing. Relax and know that you did your best for Sir Max and for Nigel, and don't worry about a thing.'

She sighed. 'I feel so much better,' she said. 'Thank you very much.'

He smiled. 'I haven't done anything,' he said.

'You have made me feel more...comfortable about things. There is a limit. I get tired very easily these days.'

Angel knew she was over eighty. 'You have done more than your share.'

The conversation closed with more pleasantries on both sides.

Angel replaced the phone thoughtfully. Mrs Dunleavy now sounded tolerably contented. It wasn't right that she had

had so much trouble. Dedicated housekeepers were worth more than…precious stones. Which made him wonder if he was ever going to find that ruby. Whether the stone turned up or not, he really must make an opportunity to go up to the convent in North Yorkshire, speak to the Mother Superior and try to trace Princess Yasmin. He needed to explain everything to her about her father and the ruby. That was the very least he must do to keep his word to Sir Max.

It took Angel a few moments to shake his mind free of the thoughts of Mrs Dunleavy, the ruby and Princess Yasmin, then he pulled the pile of post towards him. He resolved to deal with the easiest items first. That was the way to make it look as if he had done the most. It would be good for his morale.

Suddenly the phone rang again.

He reached out for the handset. A voice was speaking as he put the phone to his ear. 'I'm watching Dennis Schuster, sir.'

Angel's eyebrows shot up. It was Gawber. He was talking softly with his mouth very near the mouthpiece.

'He left his house on Edward Street in an estate car about five minutes ago,' Gawber continued, sounding chillingly uneasy. 'He drove to a big old ramshackle Victorian house at the bottom of Well Lane. I followed him and I am in my car looking at it.'

Angel's heart began to thump like the hammer on a cathedral bell. It sounded like just the place to hide somebody away.

'Can you hear me, sir?' Gawber whispered.

'Yes, Ron. Carry on.'

'Schuster looked round carefully before he let himself in. All the windows, both upstairs and down, are covered inside with either white curtains or plastic blinds. Doesn't look right.'

Angel agreed. He breathed in unevenly. 'What's it near?' he said.

'Next to a tyre depot. At the end of a very short little road called Well Lane. It's off Wakefield Road. There's not a lot of anything here.'

'Well Lane? I know it.'

'The house is in a big garden that has been let go years ago. It's all grass and nettles. It's fenced off, but there are several breaks in the fence where it has either rotted away or been damaged by vandals, and there are fields beyond.'

'Right, Ron. If he comes out, try and get a photograph, link him to the place. I'm on my way.'

Six minutes later Angel turned his BMW off Wakefield Road on to Well Lane. He saw Gawber's unmarked Ford and parked behind it. He got out of the car and glanced quickly up and down the short street. The road surface was full of pot holes and little else. The tall wood fence round the tyre depot was patched up in several places, and needed renewing and painting. The lonely silence of the scruffy place suggested that they hadn't sold a tyre for years. The properties opposite looked like garages or storehouses.

He went up to Gawber in his car and leaned into the window. 'Is he still there?'

'Yes, sir,' Gawber said.

'Right. Let's go.'

Angel followed Gawber through a side gate, along an over-grown path, which led to a tarmacked area round the house where they split forces. Angel went to the back door and Gawber made for the front. Gawber banged the knocker on the big old door and waited. He didn't wait long before he repeated the banging, and again a third time.

Angel stood just out of sight of the back door, his back against the wall. Eventually, he heard some movement, the click of a spring in a lock, the squeak of door hinges then the rattle of keys.

Angel whipped round. Dennis Schuster was on the step with his hand on the door knob.

'Good morning, sir,' Angel said. 'Can I come in?'

Schuster's eyes flashed and he sucked in air. He immediately pushed open the door, slipped inside and tried to close it, but Angel put all his weight against it. Gawber arrived and added his weight to it. The door gave way to superior authority and it was flung wide open. Angel and Gawber fell in on the floor. Schuster was thrown back against the wall. He recovered and began to run off. Angel reached out, caught him by the ankle and brought him down the length of the entrance hall.

Then Angel and Gawber got to their feet and immediately became aware of the most horrendous atmosphere. It was hot and thick and smelled of rotting cabbage. They exchanged meaningful glances; they knew exactly what it was.

The entrance hall comprised bare floorboards, bare walls and no furniture; not so much as an out-of-date calendar was to be seen.

They dashed over to Schuster, who was holding his leg and rubbing his knee.

His face was red and he was breathing quickly. 'Who are you? What do you want?' he said. 'This is a private house.'

'We're the police,' Gawber said.

Schuster glared at Angel and said, 'You're the man from the TV company!'

Angel shook his head. He pulled out his warrant card and held it up for Schuster to see. 'Detective Inspector Angel, and this is DS Gawber, Bromersley Police.'

Schuster's jaw dropped.

'Do you live here, sir?' Angel said.

'No.'

'What are you doing here then?'

'It's nothing to do with you.'

'Do you mind if we look round?'

'Have you got a search warrant?'

'We can soon get one.'

Schuster closed his eyes and opened them slowly. He looked down his nose and said, 'Well, I am afraid, dear chap, that you'll bloody well have to get one.'

'Is there anybody else in the building?'

'No.'

'Dead or alive?'

Schuster's eyes shone like a flash of lightning. '*What?* Certainly not. I want to speak to my solicitor.'

Angel said, 'Yes. I am sure you will.'

Then he turned to Gawber and nodded.

Gawber grabbed the man by the wrist, clamped on an open handcuff and said, 'Dennis Schuster, I am arresting you on suspicion of growing a Class C substance, and there may be other charges. You do not have to say anything...'

CHAPTER TEN

Gawber phoned for uniformed backup, and together with them and the prisoner, returned to the nick. Meanwhile, Angel had begun looking round the big house. There was nothing new. He had seen it all before.

It was crowded with cannabis plants. They were crammed into every possible nook and cranny, in every room and at every level. In the bathroom, they were in the bath and on top of the lavatory. They were planted in rich, moist earth in crude containers contrived from timber laths and plastic sheeting; bright lights shone on them like the Mediterranean sun; electric fans blew warm air round the house causing the greenery to wave a little here and there; a complex network of pipes, pumps, taps and tanks of water on makeshift stands irrigated the crop as required; electric cables stretched round the house like washing lines and on the floor at every doorway were bars of multiple sockets with plugs leading through thermostats to the time switches that controlled the changes. The consumption of electricity would have been enormous. Everywhere was warm, sweaty and smelled worse than the inside of an exhumation tent.

There was no sign of Selina Line or anybody else.

An hour later, Angel had completed his search and was in need of fresh air. The smell and sticky atmosphere was unpleasant. He was standing outside in the backyard. He had just tapped in the home number of DS Donald Taylor, head of SOCO, which was one of the sections not working that August Bank Holiday.

Taylor said: 'We managed to get six or seven usable photographs, sir. You were absolutely right. There's no doubt about it. The tyres of the Rolls have such a wide tread and unique tread pattern that they will be very easy to identify if you ever come across them. Anyway, I'll make up some prints and send you the photographs when I return to the office tomorrow.'

'Thank you, Don, that's great. I shall look forward to seeing the photos. But that isn't what I am phoning you about. Something else just cropped up — rather important. I have reason to believe that a woman called Selina Line may have been abducted by an ex-con called Dennis Schuster, and her life might be at risk. We have just arrested him in a large Victorian house converted into a cannabis factory, and I urgently need to know whether there is any evidence to show that Selina Line has been held on these premises, or at his home at 11 Edward Street.'

Taylor was slow to reply. 'I am in the garden, sir.'

'Yes, I thought you might be.' He realized that Don Taylor didn't want to turn out. It was Bank Holiday Monday.

'Well, how much of a risk is it, sir?' he said reasonably.

Angel bristled. He didn't like this negotiating; if he had been in Taylor's position, he would have reported for work straightaway. 'I don't know. How can I quantify it? There's no scale. It's like pain. All I can say is that the suspect is an oily smartarse, who has served time for lesser crimes. Now he seems to be getting ambitious.'

Taylor was quiet.

Angel thought he must be weakening.

'Come on, Don,' Angel said. 'You can garden anytime. Besides, you could injure yourself permanently with a spade if you're not used to it. Men in middle age need to protect their spines. You'll get paid Sunday rate and time off in lieu. You can chase the weeds away another time.'

There was a moment's delay and then Taylor said, 'I'll just get a pen, sir, and take a note of those two addresses.' That had clinched it. Angel nodded with satisfaction.

'He denies everything, sir,' Gawber said. 'Says he's never heard of her.'

Angel growled, 'Where was he on 8 August?'

'Says he can't remember.'

Angel sniffed. He ran his hand through his hair. 'I'll have a go. Come on.'

He went out of the office; Gawber followed. They went up the corridor to Interview Room Number 1.

Standing on guard outside the interview room door was DC Scrivens.

'Go find me Trevor Crisp, will you?' Angel said.

Scrivens dashed away.

In the room, seated at the table were Dennis Schuster, looking as cool as a corned beef sandwich in solitary, and Mr Bloomfield, his solicitor.

Angel nodded to both of them, switched on the recording machine, made the required statement of who was present and the date and time then said, 'Don't let's mess about, Dennis — 8 August is only seventeen days back. It was a Saturday. Two Saturdays back. It's a simple question. Where were you?'

'Don't remember, dear boy.'

'Getting married, were you?'

Schuster frowned. 'I'm already married.'

'It's called bigamy.'

'No. I'm very happily married to one lady, thank you.'

Angel wiped a hand across his mouth. 'What's the address of the other place?'

'What other place?'

'The place where you took Selina?'

'I don't know what you're talking about. My wife's name is Gloria. You obviously have me confused with somebody else.'

'You don't know Selina Line?'

'Never heard of her.'

'All right, Dennis. We'll have to do *that* the hard way. Now about the cannabis, where did you buy the plants?'

'No comment, dear boy.'

'Did you buy them locally or off the internet?'

'No comment.'

'Do you rent or own any other premises?'

'No comment.'

'Are you going to say no comment to everything I ask you?'

'No comment.'

'Schuster is far too smart to be caught out, Ron,' Angel said as he closed his office door. 'And too tough to make a confession. He's been through interviews many times before.'

'We've got to find premises where he might have taken Selina Line, sir — a place where she may still be held.'

'Indeed,' Angel said. He sat down in the swivel chair, looked up at Gawber and added, 'Unless, of course, he's telling us the truth.'

'He's very confident despite being booked for growing a Class C.'

'If it *is* him, he will make us prove everything step by step. He is not going to admit anything and make life easy. I've got Don Taylor taking a SOCO team to search that cannabis factory as well as his house. If there's any trace of Selina Line there, he'll surely find it. Nevertheless, we should take nothing for granted. We need to widen our net.'

There was a knock at the door. It was Crisp.

Angel looked up at him.

'You wanted me, sir?' Crisp said.

Angel clenched his fists. 'I'm always wanting you. Even in the middle of the night, I waken up and cry out for you!'

Gawber tried to hide a smile.

Crisp frowned. 'I don't understand —'

'Of course you don't,' Angel said. 'You never come running in here saying "I've finished that job and I've got some great news." Never. I've always got to send someone out to *find* you, then you appear with bad news.' Crisp couldn't deny it. He stood there while Angel continued the barrage. 'I sent you out with a photograph of Selina Line on Friday, to show it to every person in Bromersley authorized to marry folk, and you disappeared into outer space.'

'I've done that job, sir. I've seen them all.'

'About time. And where is he then, or she? I understand that some of them can be women these days.'

Crisp hesitated. 'There were twenty-two, sir. I've seen every one and nobody recognized her.'

Angel's eyebrows shot up and his eyes flashed. '*Nobody*?'

Crisp stood there. He didn't know what to say. There was nothing to say.

Angel put both hands to his face and rubbed his eyelids, his cheeks and then his chin. He sighed, looked back at Crisp and said, 'You'd better be sure about this.'

Crisp looked at him square on and said, 'I am sure, sir.'

Angel nodded at him, looked up at Gawber and said, 'Go to The Feathers and bring Mrs Henderson in, Ron. There's some explaining to be done.'

'Right, sir,' Gawber said and went out.

Crisp looked down at Angel, trying to look confident.

Angel opened the middle drawer of the desk and took out the three photographs of Selina Line's jewellery the insurance company had sent him. He put them on the desk and pushed them towards Crisp.

'These are expensive, very expensive pieces last seen in the possession of Selina Line. Very striking. There's a diamond and emerald necklace, an eight-carat solitaire diamond ring and a large pair of garnet earrings. There's a few quid there. £80,000 worth. See if you can spot them in the local jewellers, antique shops or auctioneers or wherever. If you do, find out how they came by them. All right?'

Crisp looked closely at the photograp

There was suddenly a very quick knc then it was thrown open with such a force t a chair that was standing against the wall beh.

It was Ahmed. He rushed in. His eyes wer dashed up to Angel sitting at the desk. 'Excuse ir,' he said, then he noticed Crisp. 'Oh, sorry, sarge. Excuse me. It's ever so important.'

'It's all right, Ahmed. I'm just going,' Crisp said. He went out and closed the door.

Angel looked at the young man closely. 'What is it, Ahmed? What's the matter?'

'Well, sir, I have just found out...that...that their eyebrows meet above their noses.'

Angel's mouth dropped open. 'What?'

'The four men, sir. You said that if I found out something that was applicable to all of them, that was the same in all four columns, you said that you would *know* why their fingers were broken.'

Angel frowned. He licked his lips.

'Well, their eyebrows meet above their noses, sir,' Ahmed said with a big smile. 'I don't know why I didn't ask them that at the beginning. Does that mean that you will now be able to work out *why*?'

Angel rubbed his chin. 'What I said was that it might *lead* to finding out why. I can't — off the top of my head — work out the...relevance, Ahmed. Not just like that.'

The smile dropped off Ahmed's face. It was the first match he had had, and he had hoped that it would have provided Angel with the clue he had needed to solve the case. Also, it would have drawn to a close the job he had found so tedious.

'I'll have to think about it, Ahmed. See what significance it has.'

Ahmed looked down at him and frowned.

'It might be a very valuable clue,' Angel said.

'Right, sir,' Ahmed said. But he knew when he was being pacified. He went out and slowly closed the door.

'Come in,' Angel said.

Gawber opened the door. His face showed that all was not well.

Angel stood up. 'Please come in, Mrs Henderson.'

She stared at him. 'I really didn't need an escort, Inspector, and to be brought to a police station as if I was a criminal.'

Gawber looked across at Angel for an indication as to whether he wanted him to stay or leave.

Despite the obvious antagonism, Angel thought he could best deal with Mrs Henderson on a one-to-one basis. He replied to Gawber with the slightest movement of his head and eyes.

Gawber went out.

Angel pointed to the chair nearest the desk. 'Please sit down, Mrs Henderson. This won't take long.'

'If you had telephoned The Feathers,' she continued, 'you could have spoken to me direct. I told you I had intended staying there until you had found Selina.'

'I'm sorry if you feel that I have been in any way discourteous,' he said. 'This is very difficult for me. You seem to be an honest woman, a woman who has her sister's best interests at heart…'

She stared across at him with piercing eyes. 'Of course I have.'

'Well, I'm afraid that everything you have told me about your sister seems to be…in error. Based on information supplied by you, I have invested considerable police time on this inquiry, Mrs Henderson. As a matter of fact, inquiries are still proceeding, but nothing so far fits the facts you supplied. You told me that it was your considered opinion that Selina would insist on being married before living with a man.'

'That is so. Yes. It is the way we were brought up.'

'She felt very strongly about this?'

'Yes. Definitely. Why?'

'Simply because we cannot find any trace of a marriage having taken place.'

She frowned.

Angel pulled open the desk drawer and took out a photograph. He pushed it across the desk at her. 'This is the photograph you gave me. Is it a true likeness of your sister, Selina Line?'

'Yes, of course. It was taken last Christmas.'

Angel rubbed his chin and said, 'No certificate of marriage has been issued to anybody looking anything like your sister during the last month or so. We have made enquiries of everybody licensed to conduct the service of marriage and none of them have seen her. You said that she had said she was to be married on 9 August?'

'That's right.'

He shook his head. 'I'm sorry, but it isn't right. Nothing's right. You said she was to be married to a teacher, who was a widower and that his name was Harry.'

'Yes. Yes. That's what she said.'

'There are no teachers in Bromersley called Harry, widower or not.'

'That's what she said. Admittedly all this was said in a rush, over the phone. I could have misheard some detail, but the essence of what she said I am certain is right.'

'Of course, she was relaying what the man had told her?'

'I suppose so. Yes.'

'Well, we can't necessarily rely on what the man told her —not if he intended to…to rob her?'

'No. Of course not.'

'But how can we separate the truth from the fiction?'

'Well, he *has* robbed her. Her bank and building society accounts are empty. I told you.'

'Those accounts could only be accessed by your sister?'

'Of course.'

'Requiring her signature, or a forged signature?'

Mrs Henderson raised her eyebrows.

Angel changed the question. 'Well, no other person's signature was required?'

'No.'

Angel reasoned that if he could uncover any direct evidence of foul play in connection with Selina Line's bank and building society accounts then it would confirm Mrs Henderson's insistence that she had been abducted. That was the next line of inquiry he must explore.

'I need the details of your sister's accounts at the bank and the building society, Mrs Henderson. There may be a lead there.'

'Of course. I have the addresses here,' she said opening her handbag. 'I don't have Selina's account numbers, but I have my own passbook for the building society and cheque book from the bank...the same institutions as Selina's.'

Angel nodded appreciatively as he took the passbook and cheque book from her. 'That's all I can think of for now. I must arrange for transport to return you to The Feathers.'

He picked up the phone and tapped in a number.

'If you would order a taxi, that would be fine,' she said.

'But we can manage to find you an unmarked car.'

'No. I'll go back by taxi.'

The phone was answered. It was Gawber.

Angel said: 'Come in, Ron.'

He replaced the phone and copied the name and addresses of the bank and building society from Mrs Henderson's books on to the back of an envelope from his inside pocket.

Gawber arrived.

Mrs Henderson took her leave of Angel, and Gawber showed her out of the office, up the corridor and past reception to the front door. He saw her into a taxi and then returned quickly down the green corridor. As he came back into the office, Angel was rubbing his ear between finger and thumb.

'Sit down a minute, Ron,' he said. 'I've been thinking. Got a little job for you. Up to now, all the evidence of the possible abduction of Selina Line has come from Mrs Josephine Henderson. We have not had an atom of substantiation from any other source. Furthermore, it was only phone calls from that phone box in Victoria Road made by Selina that connected her to this town. If we are ever going to find her, we need to find another connection between her and this town, or better still the man she's associated with who is thought to reside here, whether it is Schuster or Potter or somebody else. This might be an opportunity to make that connection. I want you to chase up Selina Line's bank and building society and see if you can make that connection. Find out how the money was withdrawn. Where it was transferred to. Who was she with at the time? And so on. All right?'

CHAPTER ELEVEN

It was 8.28 a.m. Tuesday morning. Angel was in his office. He was looking at the pile of letters and reports on his desk in front of him and wrinkling his nose. He looked at his watch. It was 8.29 a.m. He needed it to tick round another sixty seconds. The second hand moved amazingly slowly. He shook the watch to see if it had stopped. It hadn't. He noticed his fingernails. He looked at the nails on both hands. He opened the desk drawer and rummaged around among a broken pair of handcuffs, armband with 'police' printed on it, paper stapler, police whistle on silver chain, penknife, various pens, pencils, rubbers and other stationery items. He was searching for a pair of nail scissors, which he knew were there. He poked around a few times but they weren't to be seen. He frowned and slammed the drawer shut noisily. He looked again at his watch. He couldn't wait any longer. He reached over to the phone and tapped out the number.

It was answered promptly. He was surprised.

'SOLO, DS Taylor,' a voice said down the line.

'It's Michael Angel, Don. I wanted to know how you got on yesterday. Did you find any signs of the recent presence of a woman at either of those addresses?'

'Well, there was nothing apparently untoward in the house, sir. I took a few random samples but they all turned out to be those of Gloria Schuster or Dennis Schuster. The house on Well Lane seemed to contain only those of Schuster. There were no prints of females there, in the obvious places. There were no footprints available to us, nor any DNA at either property.'

Angel's jaw tightened. Again it wasn't absolute. It wasn't what he wanted to hear. It simply meant that he couldn't absolutely rule Dennis Schuster out of the Selina Line case. Why was it always impossible these days to be a hundred per cent certain of anything? Anyway, it was not Taylor's fault. SOCO had done its job. He mustn't be impatient.

'Thanks, Don,' he said and replaced the phone.

He left the office, got in his car and went down to the big house on Well Lane. A uniformed PC was standing outside the front door. He threw up a salute.

'Morning. You know what's in here, don't you?'

'Morning, sir. Yes, of course.'

'Anybody been up to the place, seen you and run off?'

'Haven't seen anybody like that, sir.'

Angel nodded. 'Keep your eyes peeled. You're not here merely to make the pictures in the papers and on the telly look good, you know.'

The constable stifled a smile.

'Is the back door locked?' Angel said.

'I have the key here, sir,' he said, producing it from his pocket.

Angel let himself into the house. The smell was awful. The heat and fan source had been switched off but there was hardly any improvement. Angel went systematically from room to room. He wanted to check whether it was possible for any room to be used as a prison cell. There were no locks on the outside of any of the rooms, nor any give-away screw holes in the doors where padlocks might have been fitted. The windows were in no way specially adapted. There were no bars across or special locks on them. A good kick and the glass would have shattered, leaving a hole large enough to escape through. There was nowhere secure enough to restrain even a frail woman — unless she was compliant or drugged. He wasn't pleased. He came out of the house, locked the door, returned the key to the PC at the front door and ambled round the house to the outbuildings. There was an outside lavatory, a coalhouse and a shelter to store logs. He looked in at all of them; they were all empty. He pursed his lips and wandered back to the PC on the door.

'Seen anything of any waste bins, lad?'

'No, sir. There aren't any.'

'They've not been whipped by the press boys, have they?'

'There weren't any when I checked in at the beginning of my shift, sir.'

He nodded, returned to his car and drove off to 11 Edward Street. There was another uniformed PC at the door. The house was unoccupied. Gloria and Trudi Schuster had found temporary accommodation with Gloria's mother. Angel looked round the small house, searching for the same things as at the Well Lane premises. He saw nothing in there that could be considered at all criminal. He came out of the house, ambled round the backyard, found a wheelie bin with a number 11 scrawled in white paint on it, and lifted the lid. It was empty except for a magazine at the bottom. He had to turn the wheelie bin upside-down to get at it. It fluttered down and flopped on to the flagstones in the backyard. He turned the wheelie bin back, put it in position and then peered down at the cover page of the magazine. It was called *Lady and Home*. He raised his eyebrows. He had come across the periodical before. He knew it to be the specialist glossy monthly magazine catering for the needs of rich, elderly people (mostly female), predominantly offering employment, also advertisers seeking to sell specialized services and products to that niche, lush market. It was standard reading for conmen looking for rich widows in big country houses to rip off.

He dashed round to his car to find an evidence bag. He pushed the magazine into it with his fingertips and sealed it.

He returned to the station, called in at SOCOs, left the copy of *Lady and Home*, told Taylor where he had found it and asked him to check through it for prints. Then he returned to his office. He was wondering what more he could do to push his inquiries about Dennis Schuster along. He couldn't think of anything. He then moved to considering whether he should chase Crisp to see how he was proceeding with searching for Selina Line's jewellery, or prod or push at further inquiries into Laurence Potter. He couldn't think of any way he could stimulate action from him while still staying the right side of Judges' Rules. He would have liked to have searched his house, but there was no possible justification he could have given to a JP to get a search warrant. Living near a particular telephone box, coming into an undetermined amount of money and having a criminal record was simply not enough.

He looked at the pile of post and reports in front of him and began fingering through the papers and envelopes.

Finding the missing Selina Line was beginning to seem impossible. He hated being beaten.

He began looking at the address and then the sender's name on the reverse side of the envelopes when his concentration slipped away. It slipped away as easily as an uneaten steamed haddock slithered into the slop bin at Strangeways. He was thinking about Selina Line and the quiet wedding to a local man, even though he was unable to find any trace of it. He imagined the bride, almost certainly not in white, middle-aged, but in a costume or, being the month of August, a summer dress, and maybe a hat. And then something occurred to him. Something important. Something that every woman would have thought of. Reality returned. He stopped fumbling with the envelopes and pushed the pile of post away. He opened a drawer and pulled out the Yellow Pages. He raced through the pages to H for hairdressers. He made extracts of the names and addresses of the six nearest to the Victoria Road telephone box, then he took a photograph of Selina Line out of his desk drawer, and dashed out of the station to his car.

He called on five hairdressers, usually one-person businesses. The lady proprietors of each business did not recognize the photograph of the missing woman. Then he stopped the BMW outside a small shop with the words 'Irene. Unisex Hairdressers' painted on the glass window. It was the last shop on his hastily scribbled list.

He sighed and wrinkled his nose. His jaw set like Dartmoor rock, he grabbed hold of the handle and walked in.

The electric bell rang and stopped when he closed the door. There were four plump, cheerful ladies in chairs around the little shop with their hair in various states of orderliness, and a slim lady in an overall with a spray can was hovering over one of them.

She was chewing something. She lowered her arm when she saw Angel standing there and smiled across at him. The jaw stopped working. 'Hello,' she said.

He smiled back. 'Sorry to bother you. Are you Irene?'

'That's me, love.'

He crossed the little room in a stride, came up very close to her, flashed his warrant card and quietly said, 'Police. Can I have a quick word, in private?'

She blinked, smiled and started chewing again. All right,' she said. 'Won't be a minute.'

Angel nodded and moved away.

She sprayed the lady in the chair with lacquer. She pointed it in all directions as if she was chasing a fly.

'There you are, Gladys. How's that?'

'That's lovely. Thank you,' Gladys said as she got out of the chair and reached for her handbag.

She gave Irene some money. The till rang.

'Same time next week?'

'Yes, please.'

'Put you in the book. Lovely,' Irene said.

Gladys left the shop. The bell rang and the door closed.

Irene looked round at the three ladies and said, 'You'll all keep a minute. Excuse me? A bit of business with this young man,' she said, with the flutter of the eyelashes and a giggle.

The three ladies smiled.

Irene looked at Angel. 'Will you come in the back?' she said with a smile.

He followed her through a door, past the bottom of a staircase, through another door into a little sitting room. He closed the door.

Her eyebrows shot up. The smile went and the chewing stopped. 'What is it? she said.

He produced the photograph. 'Nothing to worry about. Have you ever done this lady's hair?'

She took the photograph. 'I certainly wouldn't have let her out of the shop looking like that. What's it all about? Has she made a complaint about me?'

Angel felt his heart beat like the big drum in the Salvation Army. 'No. I am wanting to get in touch with her, that's all. What do you know about her?'

'What's she done? She didn't seem like a rob dog.'

'She's done nothing. I am trying to get in touch with her, that's all. When did you see her?'

'I'll have to look in my book. It must have been about three weeks ago.'

'What name did she give you?'

'I'd better get my book.'

He nodded. She went through the door back into the shop. He could hear some chatter and some laughter. She came back in with the book, smiling and chewing. She turned back several pages and eventually found it. 'The name was Line. She didn't give me her first name. Miss Line. It was for two o'clock on Friday the eight. SS, look. It was for a shampoo and set. Usual thing.'

Angel blew out an uneven sigh. He didn't want to show how elated he was. 'And what did you talk about?'

'I dunno. Very little. She didn't want to talk.'

'It's ever so important.'

'She was a quiet sort of woman. I remember now. She was not from round here.'

'Did you get the impression that she intended living round here, do you think?'

'Yes, I think she intended living round here. Yes. She wore very expensive clothes. Her shoes must have cost a hundred quid. She was a bit prim, you know. Didn't have much conversation. Very intense, she was. And in a hurry.'

'Did she say where she was staying? Talk about anybody?'

'No. She was very particular at her looking her best. Well, I wouldn't turn anybody out of the shop less than the best I could for them.'

'How did she make the appointment?'

'By phone, I think.'

'Do you have an address or a phone number?'

She looked in the book. 'No.' She frowned 'That's funny,' she said. 'I *always* take a phone number.'

Angel rubbed his chin. 'Supposing she said she was ringing from a phone box…'

Irene smiled. 'That's it. That's what she said. I wouldn't bother with taking that, would I? No point.'

'And how did she get here? Who brought her or did she drive herself? This is very important.'

Irene shook her head. 'I don't know. She just came through the door, on her own.'

'And left in the same fashion? Nobody with her? Nobody called for her?'

'No. She was on her own.'

'Did she mention any names? Did she talk about her husband?' he said, watching her closely.

'No. But I did notice she wasn't wearing a wedding ring or any ring on that hand, for that matter. It's funny, I tend to look for rings on that third finger, left hand. I'm a nosy devil. She was wearing a monster diamond solitaire on her right hand, though. Beautiful thing. Must have been ten carats. Probably not real. I'm not wearing one either,' she said with a grin. 'You might have noticed. He hopped it years ago. Only good thing he ever did.'

Angel licked his lips. 'Irene, is there anything else you can tell me...about what she said, what she wore, her plans, anything, absolutely anything at all?'

'I don't think so. She just wasn't talkative. She was shy, you know? I'm right nosy, but I couldn't get to know anything.' She chewed a few times and then said, 'No, I really cannot think of a single thing. As I said, she was in a hurry.'

'Well, thank you very much. That's been most helpful.' He pulled a card out of his top pocket and gave it to her. 'If you remember anything else — however small — please contact me at that number.'

Irene took the card, stopped chewing, smiled, wriggled her shoulders, came much closer and said, 'Here. Now. You're not leaving without telling me what she's done, are you?'

It was a quarter to five. Angel walked into the office, whistling the theme from one of his eight gramophone records. His step was lighter. He no longer felt that he had a brick on his chest. He pulled open a drawer in the desk, took out his address book, riffled through the pages, found a number, picked up the phone and tapped out the number of The Feathers.

'Mrs Henderson? I'm glad I've caught you in. I thought you'd be pleased to know that I've found positive evidence that your sister *was* in Bromersley on Friday 8 August.'

He heard her sigh then she said, 'Oh, Inspector, that's great news. Is she all right? Have you found her? Do you know where she is now?'

'I'm afraid not. Although we cannot find *where* the marriage took place, or even if it *did* take place, the fact that your sister had her hair attended to on the eighth tends to confirm that she had expected to get married the following day.'

'Oh? Well. Yes, I suppose it does.'

He told her of his inquiries at the hairdressers and the essence of what Irene had told him.

'Oh, Inspector, I am so delighted. I was afraid that you must have thought that I was mistaken, and that I had got the dates wrong.'

Angel said nothing.

'I will sleep better tonight,' she added.

They ended their call and he replaced the phone.

He rubbed his chin. It was a great step forward. But he needed to find out where Selina Line was at that time. His eyes caught the pile of stuff on his desk. He looked up at the clock. It was five minutes to five. He wrinkled his nose. Hardly worthwhile starting anything. He looked at the heap a moment longer. His sense of honesty began to overtake his common sense, and he reached out to it.

The phone rang.

He pulled back his hands with a grin, swivelled round in the chair, snatched up the phone and spoke into the mouthpiece. 'Angel.'

It was an old snout of his who always gave the name of Helpman. Angel had never known his real name. It didn't matter. His information had always been reliable.

Helpman sounded more excited than usual. 'I got a hundred quid's worth, Mr Angel, and no mistake,' he said.

'I can't pay out that sort of money, Mr Helpman. You know that.'

A new police form had been devised (one of many) and Angel had to give details of the information received, the amount spent and the informant's full name and address before Harker would have authorized the chitty for reimbursement. If Angel had asked Helpman for his name and address he would have run off and never been seen again, and some of his cases may never have been solved. He had christened him Helpman and the address he gave was of a flat in London that had existed years back but was now pulled down for road widening. He didn't expect anyone to follow it up.

'What I know is really worth a ton to you, honest, Mr Angel.'

'Sorry, Mr Helpman.'

There was silence.

Angel said, 'Are you there?'

'Yeah. Yeah,' the man said. He was distinctly cooler. 'Eighty nicker?'

'Fifty is tops. You know *that*. I've told you that before. And *I've* got to be the arbiter of its value. Who knows, I might already know what you have for me.'

'Yeah,' he said sneeringly. 'You've been very tight in your pay-outs just lately.'

'No. No.'

Then with a tremor in his voice, Helpman said, 'You have no idea of the risks I take.'

'I've always been as generous as I can be. And as discreet. You know that I have never disclosed my source.'

'My life could be on the line if *this* leaked out, I tell you.'

Angel's eyes narrowed. He thought he must have something very special. Helpman had never actually used that phrase before.

'Are you at the usual place?'

'Yes.'

'I'll leave straightaway.'

Angel replaced the phone, made for the green corridor, past the cells and outside to the BMW. He drove into the town centre then out on the Huddersfield Road via a back way to where a low railway bridge passed over the road. He looked round for somewhere to stop; the only place was just under the bridge. He got out of the car and walked back to a little newsagent's around the corner. He dashed in, bought an *Evening Star* and returned to the car. He put it on the seat beside him, and then drove off quickly towards Tunistone. When he was out of the built-up area, he glanced over his shoulder at the tartan car rug wedged between the back and front seats. It twitched from time to time.

'You can come up now,' Angel said.

'Anybody following us?' Helpman said.

Angel glanced again in the mirror. 'No.'

Helpman threw off the car rug, edged up into the back seat, pressed his head back into the corner and kept his face well away from the windows.

'Phew. I think I am getting too old for this game, Mr Angel. Have you brought the money?'

'What have you got, Mr Helpman?' he said, pressing his foot on the accelerator as he passed the speed de-restriction signs. They were moving into the countryside.

'I'll get straight to the point, Mr Angel. I visited an old friend of mine the other day. He'd just come out of Boston, worked his way through Lincoln, and while he was in Boston he was on the same corridor as Aaron Moss — played pinball together — who happened to mention the long-standing vendetta between your Charlie Drumme and the Corbetts.'

'Is Aaron Moss a relation of Cecil Moss?'

'His brother. Now, Aaron said that he was going straight when he'd finished his time in Boston. He'd a little boy, five or six, and he wanted to see him grow up. Anyway he'd been approached — indirectly — by Charlie Drumme to get shot of the Corbetts once and for all. They are a vicious couple of brothers from Manchester.'

'I know them. I've met the Corbetts.'

'Oh? Well, Charlie Drumme meant with shooters. *Shooters*, Mr Angel. Anyway, Aaron said he wanted nothing of it, but he knew of a man who would do it, smooth as a cat's belly. What the intermediary didn't know, Mr Angel, was that Aaron hated the sight of Charlie Drumme. So why should he do him any favours? It was partly Drumme who got him into so much trouble with the coppers in Manchester. Years ago he ran off a job leaving Aaron carrying the money when the coppers turned up. But that's a long story. Now, although Aaron and Cecil are brothers, they're not that close. Nevertheless, I reckon Aaron told Cecil, and he told James and Lloyd Corbett, which probably served to fuel the ding-dong between Charlie Drumme and the Corbetts. But that's by the way. It's been going on for a year or so. I won't charge you for that. This is the big one. Who do you think Charlie has set on to get rid of the Corbetts, Mr Angel?'

'I don't know.'

'The Fixer. Yus.'

Angel's eyes narrowed. He had to concentrate on his driving.

'And Charlie is paying him ten grand,' Helpman continued. 'That's for the both of them. Now, The Fixer insists he wants to take them out together. That is, he wants them in the same place at the same time. He wants to make one job of it. Economical. And he don't want to risk one getting away and coming hunting for him.'

'When and where is this showdown to take place?'

Helpman's mouth turned down. His eyes shone. 'I don't know *that*, Mr Angel. Whew! How would I know *that*?'

'And who is The Fixer?'

'I don't know.'

'Well, I can't do much only knowing the intention that Drumme has set The Fixer on. I can't arrest somebody I don't know, for intending to murder two men at an unknown place at an unknown time, can I? You'll have to do better than that, Mr Helpman.'

'Isn't it enough that you *know*? You can warn the Corbetts that they should be out of here.'

'I would have to arrest The Fixer.'

'Arrest him? Huh.' He turned up his nose. 'You wouldn't get near him.'

Angel's eyes narrowed. 'What's his *real* name, Mr Helpman?'

'I don't know, Mr Angel, and if I did know, I'd have to emigrate to Mars, and even that might not be far enough away from him for me to stay alive.'

Through the driving mirror, Angel saw genuine fear in his eyes. It seemed to happen to everybody when the name The Fixer was mentioned. Angel ran his hand through his hair.

'At least give me an approximation of when this is likely to happen.'

'Oh, soon. Very soon. Could be tonight, could be tomorrow, or —'

'Yeah. Yeah. This week, next week, sometime, never. I can't work like that.'

Helpman's face dropped. He could see that Angel was not that impressed. The darting around of his eyes showed he was desperately thinking of something to say that would make more of the information he had to offer.

Angel was thinking quickly to make the most of Helpman before they parted.

From out of the blue, Angel said, 'Where's big Laura these days?'

'If James Corbett is in the town, she'll be there, hustling girls, wherever they are.'

Angel knew he was right. That stuck with him. He had an idea.

Thereafter was an uncomfortable few moments. Helpman was embarrassed. He realized he had not impressed Angel with his information. He couldn't see him getting the £50 he had expected. Angel was disappointed. He clearly thought Helpman had more information to give and was holding back.

He swiftly banged the indicator stalk on the steering column and turned right; shortly afterwards he did the same again. It put him on a parallel road back to town. 'I'm sorry, Mr Helpman. Twenty-five is all that's worth. Give me the name of The Fixer and the time and place of the would-be attack and I could do you fifty pounds straight off'

Helpman sighed. 'That would be worth a *hundred*.'

'Maybe,' Angel said with a shrug.

'You're a hard man, Mr Angel,' he said, but secretly he was satisfied with the deal.

Angel paid him the cash as they travelled, then he drove the BMW back to the gloomy privacy provided by the low bridge. As soon as the wheels stopped moving, Helpman dived out of the car and disappeared into obscurity faster than a teenager with money.

Angel moved away from under the bridge swiftly and drove straight to Bromersley market. He went to a woman he knew who sold costume jewellery. He gave her £25 and bought a dozen or more 16" gold-plated chain necklaces. She put them in a blue plastic bag and handed them to him.

He went back to the office. There was a lot to do. He summoned Gawber, briefed him and then sent him home. He phoned the Firearms Support Unit at Wakefield and spoke to his old friend DI Waldo White. Then he went home, had an early tea and went to bed.

CHAPTER TWELVE

It was 2 a.m. on Canal Road in the rundown area of Bromersley. The night sky was as black as fingerprint ink.

The BMW rolled slowly along the cobbled street, through high-walled, empty warehouses and under age-stained arches with the words 'Robinson's Repository and Removals' painted in big letters over everywhere. In every alleyway, doorway, niche, nook and recess, the car headlights picked out pairs of skinny legs, white as chip fat, supporting skimpily dressed bodies with naked middles and topped with a fuzz or length of dark or fair hair. Each girl, one after another, turned her head, pulled back her shoulders, tightened her buttocks, shielded her eyes, took a rapid suck on a cigarette and tottered in uncomfortable high heels towards the car.

Angel hated raising the expectations of the drug-hungry women. He wasn't wanting what they were offering. But he *was* looking for a woman. A very specific woman. He didn't know what she looked like. All he knew was her name. And she was likely to be somewhere more comfortable than standing half-naked on unfriendly flagstones in the middle of the night.

He speeded up the car and drove to the end of Canal Road, turned round and pulled on the handbrake. He took off his tie, put it in his pocket and unbuttoned the top button of his shirt. He opened the glove compartment and pulled out a vacuum flask, plastic food container, yellow duster and the blue plastic bag. He poured himself a full cup of coffee, then opened the plastic box and looked in it to see what there was. His dear wife Mary had prepared two brown bread sandwiches of ham and beetroot, which he ate pretty quickly, and she had included a Golden Delicious apple. He looked at it, smiled as he thought of her, and put it in his pocket for later. He finished off the cup of coffee and screwed on the top, pleased that there would be some for later. He covered the RT with the duster, carefully tucking it safely round the handset. He opened the blue bag, took out the rolled gold necklaces and put them over his head and round his neck one at a time until he sparkled like a Christmas tree at Hamleys. He turned down the driving mirror, looked in it, nodded and put it back in position. He put the BMW into gear and rolled the car slowly along, passing two or three girls until he was about halfway along Canal Road. He stopped and a girl teetered towards the car. He pressed the button and the car window rolled down.

'Hello there, darling,' she said, peering through the window. 'Looking for a good time?'

Angel switched on the inside light and looked across at her. Her face was highly coloured with carmine and rouge. Her eyes were dull, her mouth moist and always open. Her hair was long, black at the roots turning to bleached sisal. She must have been pretty sometime, but tonight she had the allure of a fridge.

He screwed up his face. 'I've been sent by Charles Drumme — Mr Drumme to you — to sort out big Laura,' he said, giving his best Cagney impression. 'Where is she?'

The girl stared at him and gasped. Her jaw dropped. 'Frigging hell,' she said.

She turned away from the car and yelled out, 'Hey, girls. This ain't a frigging punter. Come from Charlie Drumme. He's looking for big Laura.'

Girls ran up to her from every direction. There was a crowd of eight or ten girls in a huddle on the pavement in a few seconds.

'What you on about?'

'This frigging bloke is looking for big Laura.'

There were gasps and calls of 'Oh my god' echoing round the dark cobbles.

They chattered and chirped for a few moments. One of them broke away from the huddle, came up to Angel's car window, glared at him and with a curled lip said, 'Well, who the frigging hell *are* you?'

'I'm from Mr Drumme and I want big Laura,' he said. 'Where is she?'

She turned back to the huddle.

'He says he's from Charlie Drumme,' she said.

There was more animation from the huddle.

A dozen or more others had joined in the meeting. They yelled and screamed at each other for a few moments. Then they suddenly all turned and looked towards the car. They came nervously up to the window. Those at the front peered in, looked round the inside of the car and then looked closely at him.

One of them said: 'Are you really from Charlie Drumme?'

'Yes,' Angel shouted. 'Mr Drumme is taking you back.'

'Are you going to collect for him, then?'

'No. I'm just here to get rid of big Laura and the Corbetts.'

There was stunned silence.

Angel suddenly said in a loud voice: 'If you don't tell *me* where I can find her, Mr Drumme will come down himself.'

'Charlie Drumme's in the hospikle,' another said.

'He gets out tomorrow. He's as good as new,' Angel said.

They turned away and went into a huddle again. It didn't take long. They returned to the window. The first girl came back up to the window.

'Big Laura. She ain't frigging here. But she comes down most frigging nights, though.'

'What time? What time?' he snapped.

'Huh. When she frigging wants,' the girl said. Then she added, 'If you go away round the block, we can give you a bell when she comes.'

'Yes. Yes,' many voices called out enthusiastically. Some girls screamed. In the reflection of the car headlights, he saw several jump up and down, waving their hands.

'All right,' Angel growled. 'How will I know her?'

'She's in a frigging big silver Mercedes, SL55,' the second girl said.

'You don't see many of them around here,' another girl added.

He scribbled his mobile number on a margin of the *Evening Star* he had bought earlier, tore it off and gave it to the first girl. 'There's my number. Don't mess me up,' he said sternly, 'or I'll come back for you.'

'It'll cost you a tenner,' she said, licking her lips nervously. Angel growled, peeled off a ten pound note from his money roll, and gave it to her.

He heard a voice in the dark say, 'You should've said a hundred.'

With shaking hands the girl snatched it, kissed it and said, 'Don't worry. I won't mess you up. I'd do anything to get that frigging bitch off my back.'

Angel sighed. He would be glad when this particular night's work was over.

He switched off the interior light of the car, closed the near-side window and then released the handbrake. The BMW glided quickly away to the end of Canal Road; he turned first right and right again. It took him on to Sebastopol Terrace, an old terraced row of houses without street lights. All the houses were in darkness except for one bedroom where some poor soul no doubt couldn't get to sleep. He drove the car down the street to a frontage of shops with a pub, The Fisherman's Rest, in the middle. The pub had a small car park at the side. No vehicles were on it. He drove on to the car park, pulled on the brake and turned off the ignition. He took his mobile out of his pocket and tapped in a number.

It was soon answered.

'Ron,' Angel said. 'It's all set. Has Waldo White and his team arrived?'

'Yes, sir. Eight men in two Range Rovers. They've been showing me their new Heckler and Koch G36s. They only weigh 7.28 lbs.'

'Good. I don't care what they weigh as long as they can shoot straight with them. Pick me up on the corner of Sebastopol Terrace and Wakefield Road, ASAP.'

'Right, sir.'

He closed the phone and dropped it in his pocket. He got out of the BMW, locked it and began the walk along the street towards the main road. Apart from the distant hum of traffic on the M1, it was so quiet you could have heard the crystals in a breathalyser change colour.

A distant clock chimed three. It took him only two minutes to reach the main road, which was well illuminated. He kept back in the shadow behind the corner of the end house and waited.

There was very little traffic on the main road — a big ASDA articulated wagon and a red post office van that looked brown in the halogen lights passed, then an unmarked Ford car he recognized. It was Gawber. Angel stepped out of the shadow and flagged him down. He got in the nearside seat.

'Take this corner and park up,' he said, indicating Sebastopol Terrace.

Gawber took the corner, stopped in the street, switched off the lights and turned off the engine.

'Where are Waldo White and his men?' Angel said.

'Two streets up, sir. They're raring to go.'

Angel nodded then rubbed his chin. He realized he needed a shave. He was silent for a moment. 'They don't like being pimped by a woman,' he said.

Gawber nodded. 'You said that you thought that would be the case.'

'They'd rather be bullied by Charlie Drumme than this Laura woman. One of the girls is ringing me on my mobile when big Laura appears. As my car will now be clocked in by the girls, I want us to follow her in your car. All right?'

'What's big Laura's car?'

'A big silver Mercedes. SL55.'

Gawber looked impressed.

Suddenly ahead of them they heard a small explosion and a huge red and yellow flickering light illuminated the side of the high warehouses on Canal Road on their left behind the house roofs.

'What the hell was that?' Gawber asked.

Angel thought it came from somewhere in the middle of Sebastopol Terrace. His pulse rocketed. He gasped. 'Oh hell! It's my car.'

Gawber looked at him. His big eyes reflected the yellow light.

'*They've fired my bloody car*!' Angel said.

Gawber started the car engine.

Angel's mobile went.

'Just a minute, Ron,' he said as he dived in his pocket. He switched on the phone and spoke into it. 'Hello, yes.'

Nobody spoke. The line sounded alive, but nobody spoke.

'Hello. Are you there?' Angel said.

There was still no voice.

'Speak up,' he said. 'There's nothing to be afraid of.'

There was a small cough. 'It's me,' a small female voice said.

'Is big Laura there now?'

'Yes.'

'In her usual car?'

'Yes.'

'On her own?'

'Yes.'

'Right. Now carry on as usual. Act normal. All right?'

The girl said, 'Yes.'

He closed the phone and turned to Gawber. 'Turn round smartly, Ron, and go down Canal Road.'

As Gawber swung the car into reverse, Angel tapped triple nine on the mobile. It was answered by an emergency telephonist. He quickly reported the Sebastopol Terrace explosion to the Fire Service. Then he cancelled the connection and tapped in another number.

It was answered after only half a ring. 'Waldo White.'

'Michael Angel. Are you all set?'

White sighed. 'I thought you'd forgotten us, Michael,' he said with a grin in his voice.

'We are in a blue unmarked Ford Mondeo, Waldo. Please come in when I shout for you.'

'Right. Can you keep this line open…give me a commentary…so that I'll know what's happening…and we'll know what to expect? I'll hold on.'

'Yes…all right. We are going into Canal Road now.'

Gawber drove the Ford slowly along, girls appearing every twenty yards or so.

Angel said: 'It's very dark. Don't expect street lights… there aren't any. There are lots of girls standing about. There are two kerb crawlers, and there's one car standing…a girl leaning forward, negotiating with a client. No sign yet of big Laura's car…we're nearly at the end of the road.'

In the headlights, suddenly it appeared.

Angel gasped. So did Gawber.

'It's *there*!' they cried out in unison.

A big low-slung luxury silver car with an unmistakable Mercedes logo and model code SL55 was standing at the side of the road. Two girls were at the nearside window talking to a figure in the driving seat; it was too dark to see what was happening.

Angel's pulse began to bang in his ears.

'You've got it?' Waldo White said.

'Staring straight at it,' Angel said. 'Ron's going to drive straight past slowly. Its index number is Yankee, Mike, Zero, Eight, Mike, X-Ray, X-Ray.'

White said: 'Got it.'

'We're driving up to the end of the road, turning round and parking up.'

'Don't lose it, Michael,' White said.

Angel knew it was vital not to let the Mercedes slip away. It was a powerful car with a lot of horses under its bonnet.

Gawber turned the Ford round, stopped at the side of the road and switched off the lights. Angel and Gawber looked ahead. There was nothing to see. It was as if someone had covered the windscreen with a black curtain.

'I'll get out,' Angel said.

Gawber didn't like it. 'Be careful.'

'We'll come down and take the Mercedes, Michael.' White said. 'Stay where you are.'

'No. We want the Corbetts as well,' Angel said, getting out of the car.

'I'll come with you, sir,' Gawber said.

Angel put his hand over the mouthpiece. 'No, Ron. Can't risk anything happening to *this* car. We're going to need it to follow the Merc. Stay with it.'

'I won't know what's going on,' Gawber said.

'That's all right. I'll come back here, won't I?' he said and closed the car door.

Gawber frowned. He wasn't happy about it.

Angel heard White through the earpiece say: 'What's happening, Michael, I can't hear you.'

Angel took his hand off the mouthpiece. 'It's all right, Waldo. There was nothing to say because there's nothing to see. I'm going to creep up to the Merc on foot… If it moves off, I'll give you the shout.'

'Right. Be careful.'

'Nothing to be careful about. There's nothing and nobody here… It's just…blackness…brick walls, in places, surfaced with concrete. I am on the pavement, such as it is. The council should be ashamed of themselves. There are more potholes than a seaside putting green. Hmmm. I can smell burning rubber. My car, probably. In the next street.

Harker will go mad. Aaah. I can see the lights of a car ahead. Just the sidelights.'

'Don't get too near, if you think it's the Mercedes.'

'There are lots of ginnels and alleyways. I can dodge into one if I want to hide. I wish I had brought a torch.'

'Is it the Merc, Michael? Is it the Merc?'

'Can't tell. Probably. Get a bit nearer… Hang on… Yes, it is. There's a crowd of girls round it now.'

White said: 'That's near enough. Back off, Michael. Back off'

'It's all right. I might be able to hear what's happening.'

'Don't go too close, Michael.'

Angel edged a little further along the pavement. Then he froze. For a brief moment he couldn't move. Out of his eye corner he saw something or somebody move. He didn't know what. He sucked in a deep breath. Then everything happened quickly. Someone had stepped out of the doorway behind him and jabbed something hard in his right kidney.

'Mr Angel. I thought it must be you.'

It was Lloyd Corbett.

Angel turned quickly, dropped the mobile, jabbed Corbett in the stomach with his elbow, causing him to bend forward, then at the same time as he reached to his side for the weapon, he landed a mighty upper cut under Corbett's chin with his left. The gun went off He heard screams from the girls. He felt a searing pain in his side. Corbett landed on his back on the cobbles, still holding the gun. Angel saw him point it at him and gave a swing at it with his foot. Corbett screamed. The gun went off again. There was a flash of light. There were more screams. The gun rattled along the cobblestones.

Three kerb crawlers raced away out of Canal Road, their lights illuminating the scene and flashing on to the gun as they flew past.

Angel reached down quickly to retrieve it.

A commanding voice he did not recognize said, 'Leave that gun where it is if you want to live, Inspector.'

He stopped, turned his head in the direction of the Mercedes and saw the silhouette of somebody enormous standing in front of the lights: he reasoned it must be female because of the unusual outline of a hat with some sort of flower decoration on it.

'Put up your hands,' she said. She had a voice like coke grating under a cellar door.

He could see the glint of a gun being thrust forward, assertively, waist high.

He was panting. His heart was racing. He straightened up, leaving Corbett's gun in the gutter. Then he realized that this must undoubtedly be big Laura. She *was* big. Also he noticed a dozen or so girls behind her and grouped around the Mercedes.

Then there was some movement at the side of him. Lloyd Corbett was getting to his feet. He was opening and closing his hand repeatedly, trying to bring life and normality back into it. He glanced at Angel and muttered, 'You bastard. You frigging bastard. You'll pay for this.'

Angel feared that he might. His stomach was in turmoil. His head was banging, his pulse racing, his breathing fast and uneven. His side hurt: it was a searing pain. He couldn't imagine how serious it was. He wasn't used to this sort of rough and tumble. He thought he had left all this behind when he became an inspector twelve years ago. He licked his lips as he stood there with his hands up. He wondered what they were going to do with him next. He saw Lloyd Corbett bend down and recover the gun. It was small with black plastic grips and seemed to have a blue look about it. He thought it was a Beretta. It might be small, he thought, but at point-blank range it was as deadly as any other gun.

Corbett checked over the gun as he went across to the woman.

'Let's get rid of him,' she said quietly.

'Yeah. Yeah,' Corbett said wearily, without thinking.

'Angel,' she said. 'Move across to that wall.'

Angel wondered what she intended to do.

She waggled the gun to hurry him on.

Angel's lips tightened against his teeth. He could see that she was wearing a plain dress with a plain coat of similar colour, a large hat, the sort of thing worn at Ascot, and plain high-heeled leather shoes. She was very tall, and oversize in every dimension. He guessed her age might be around forty. If it wasn't for the receding hairline, Lloyd Corbett might have seemed like her son.

Angel moved where he was directed. But he didn't like the way events were developing. He noticed his mobile phone still open on the pavement not far from him. He would have liked to have picked it up. But it would have to stay there.

'Now turn round and face the wall,' she said.

He hesitated.

'Hurry up,' she snapped.

His blood turned cold. His bowels turned to water. If he was about to die, at least he would like to see the person pulling the trigger.

Lloyd Corbett turned to her. 'No. Not here,' he whispered. He nodded towards the girls behind them. Too many witnesses.'

Laura wasn't pleased. After a moment, she nodded.

Angel sighed the sigh of his life. His thoughts were everywhere. How was he going to get out of this? What about Waldo White? What about Ron Gawber? Where were they?

Laura turned round to the girls. 'Get back to work, you bitches. Get some frigging money earned. This isn't a bloody sideshow.'

The girls muttered something and then quickly disappeared into the blackness.

Angel couldn't believe that he was the prisoner of a Corbett and this dreadful woman. And where was James Corbett? He expected him to turn up at any second.

Lloyd Corbett looked at Laura, nodded towards Angel and said: 'He won't be on his own, Laura. Let's get out of here!' She nodded.

'We'll have to take him with us,' Corbett said.

Her eyes flashed like a wild cat in the night. 'A frigging copper in my car?' she said.

Corbett shrugged. 'Watch him while I open the door.'

She was pleased to be in a position to shoot him, particularly as now there weren't any witnesses. Angel knew it. He stood there motionless: he was not going to give her any excuse.

Corbett dashed up to the car and opened the nearside front door.

The inside of the car lit up like an operating theatre.

He dug the muzzle of the gun in Angel's back and said, 'Get in

Laura frowned. 'In the front, Lloyd?' she said.

'Don't worry. I'll sit right behind him with this on his neck,' he said, waving the Beretta.

Angel climbed inside. As he leaned back, he felt the searing pain of the gunshot in his side. He put his hand to it and felt blood. He said nothing.

'No tricks,' Corbett said as he climbed in behind him.

The cold steel in the back of his neck caused Angel to focus his mind most remarkably. He could hardly think of anything else.

Laura opened the door. In a sort of a dream, he saw her take her handbag from the glove compartment to the right of the steering wheel, drop in her gun, fasten it with the clasp and replace the bag in the glove compartment. He clocked in that it was too far away and too well buttoned up for him to reach even if a chance came up.

Laura got in the car. It rocked down at the offside with her weight.

Angel watched her. She had curves all right. She had a stomach that was one big curve, outwards. Her bosom was so big she could have suckled for Yorkshire.

She closed the door and the inside of the car was in darkness.

For some inexplicable reason, Angel preferred the dark. It seemed more secure.

'Let's get away from here,' Corbett said. 'You don't know who is around.'

'Yeah. Yeah,' she said.

She turned the ignition key and the engine began to hum. She engaged gear, released the handbrake and the car flew over the cobblestones along Canal Road. The headlights caught several girls in its path on the way. They reached the main road in two seconds and turned left towards Wakefield.

It was a main road out of town and restricted to thirty miles per hour, and Laura was keeping exactly to it. There was very little traffic.

After a mile or so, Angel noticed that the muzzle of the gun was no longer at his neck. He gave an involuntary sigh. One slip of Corbett's finger and he would have been dead. Angel heard the gentle tapping out on the keyboard of a telephone, then he heard Lloyd's voice: 'It's me… I know, I know, we had a bit of trouble, James… That copper, Angel, turned up… He was snooping round… No, he was on his own… Of course I'm sure… He was on his own talking to one of the girls, waving his badge around, trying to get a free jump, I expect… We got rid of his car… I don't know, James, do I?' he suddenly said angrily. 'Anyway, we're bringing him to the farm now… All right. Don't lose your frigging wig… *We couldn't help it*! Canal Road was buzzing… What could we have done with him? *We had no choice*!' he yelled.

Angel heard a click. It sounded as if the conversation had ended abruptly and that James Corbett wasn't pleased about Lloyd and Laura taking him to their place of hiding. But Angel had learned one thing: their destination was a farm.

The feel of cold metal returned to the back of his neck, sending a cold chill to his mind and down his spine.

Laura glanced back at Lloyd Corbett and said, 'What's the matter with James, then?' Laura said.

'Aw. He don't want the copper at the farm,' Lloyd Corbett said.

Laura didn't reply.

Angel watched her drive. She was a very competent driver and the car was moving along at a good speed since they had passed the speed de-restriction signs and were out of the built-up area. He knew the road well enough. They must now be about ten miles from Wakefield. He wondered what had happened to Ron Gawber and Waldo White. He couldn't turn round to see if they were following. He desperately hoped that they were. It was his only possibility of getting out of this mess, and the only chance of catching the Corbetts and Laura and whoever else was awaiting him at the farm.

Laura said: 'You know, Lloyd, we can't stay there for ever. Don't James think it's time for a move?'

'Yeah, but it's a good place. It's safe.'

'We could put the copper in the barn, and leave him there.'

'Yeah, but where would we move to?'

The car suddenly slowed.

Laura knocked a switch on the steering column; amber lights flashed on the left. Angel saw a crude sign painted in black on wood at the side of the road with an arrow that read 'Heartbreak Farm'.

A chill ran down Angel's back as he wondered what was ahead of him.

Laura turned the steering wheel left and the car bonnet pointed down a cart track, hardly noticeable from the main road. The track continued for half a mile, over a railway bridge through a field, past three barns or farm buildings and quite suddenly a large modern house partly covered in ivy appeared opposite the last one. The tyres crunched noisily on the silver-grey gravelled drive.

There were lights in most of the large windows. Lights came on illuminating a patio area as they arrived, and the front door opened. A big figure in a silk dressing gown walked down the stone steps. It was James Corbett. He was carrying a glass with a drink in it. He glared at the car as it came to a stop in front of him.

Angel noted that the muzzle of the gun had been removed from the back of his neck. He breathed out a long sigh silently. He noticed that his back was stinging. It must still be bleeding. He licked his lips. His jaw tightened. He must appear strong and in perfect control.

James Corbett walked down the steps from the patio as Laura applied the handbrake. The car stopped at his feet, noisily spraying some of the gravel. He glared at Angel and pointed to him as Lloyd Corbett leaped out of the back door.

"You stupid nerk,' James Corbett said.

Lloyd shrugged. 'What choice had I?' he said.

Then James Corbett turned back to the house and yelled: 'Mossy! Mossy, where are you? Take care of him.'

Angel saw Moss rush out of the house with an old Sten gun on a strap over his shoulder and carrying a torch. He ran down the steps, pointing the gun in the direction of the car. Angel shook his head in dismay. It seemed that the place was armed to the gunnels. He was going to be lucky to get out of this alive.

The brothers walked up the steps together, arguing and shouting at each other.

Laura withdrew the ignition key, picked up her handbag and got out of the car.

James Corbett looked back at her and said: 'Are you all right, love? Apart from this frigging idiot brother of mine, did anybody else get out of line?'

'They wouldn't dare,' she said, slamming the car door.

'What's the take?'

She waved her handbag and pulled a face like a Cheshire cat. 'Over two grand.'

He waved his hands in the air. He looked at Lloyd and said, 'I knew it was worth it. What did I tell you? There's brass here. Manchester's played out.' He turned back to her. 'Give Mossy a hand with the copper, Laura, love, will you?'

Her eyes glinted in the moonlight.

'Oh yes,' she said, and she rubbed her hands together as she crunched across the gravel.

James Corbett turned back to her. 'But don't hurt him,' he said.

She flashed her eyes angrily at him but he didn't see; he was talking animatedly to Lloyd.

In the few moments that Angel had not been closely watched, he had reached into his pocket, taken out the Golden Delicious apple and concealed it in his hand.

Moss came up to the nearside front door of the Mercedes, opened it and flashed the torch.

'Get out,' he said.

Laura took the gun out of her handbag and watched Moss prod Angel towards the building opposite the house. They trudged over, kicking through the silver-grey gravel. The door was wedged open with a brick.

Moss flashed the torch inside. Angel glanced quickly round. It was simply an empty barn with three centre posts in a line supporting the roof. There was a row of hooks on the wall of the barn near the door. Hanging from it were lengths of leather straps, horse collars and rope. The owners presumably had had an interest in horses.

Laura followed them inside.

'What did James tell you to do with him?' she said.

'Tie him up to that post and tie him up real tight,' he said.

'I'll watch him while you do it, Mossy,' she said, waving her gun in Angel's direction.

Moss flashed the light. He unthreaded several lengths of rope from the hook, selected one and put the others back. He then turned back to Angel. 'Up against that post, copper,' he said.

Angel had no option but to do as he was told.

'Hurry up, Mr Angel,' Laura said. 'Hands behind your back.'

'Hold the torch, Laura,' Moss said.

Angel looked at the big hand confidently holding the gun and the torch in front of him about eight feet away. He wasn't planning taking any risks.

Moss busied himself behind Angel with the rope.

'You know, he'd make good target practice, Mossy,' she said.

Angel's pulse started up again. What on earth could she mean? His pulse banged louder than the big drum in Dodworth Colliery Band.

Moss pulled hard at the rope as he made the first knot. He didn't want to hear what else she had to say.

She frowned, looked at Angel and said: 'Yes. You know what, Mossy? I've always wanted to see if I could shoot somebody's earlobe off. Well, both earlobes, really. You know, to match.'

Angel couldn't imagine anything more humiliating, and the pain would surely be hard to bear.

'If I could do that,' she continued, 'I should think I would be regarded as a top shot…and a woman at that…and in the light only of a torch.'

'No,' Moss said, his eyes darting in all directions. 'No. You're not to harm him.'

'I saw it in an old film once.'

'You're not to harm him. You heard what James said.'

'I don't care what he said.'

Footsteps could be heard in the gravel. A figure appeared out of the darkness through the open door.

'You don't care what I said?' James Corbett growled. He was holding a gun and pointing it casually in front of him.

Laura said: 'Didn't hear you coming, James. I was only…fooling around.'

'If we get rid of this copper we have to do it right,' James Corbett said. 'Leave no trace that it has anything to do with us. It needs some thinking about. Planning. You understand?'

Moss suddenly turned from Angel, held up a wet, red hand and said: 'Phew. There's some blood here, boss.'

'Where's that from?'

'His side. Look, his coat is covered. He's bleeding.'

Laura shone the torch at Angel's back. Her face changed. Her lips tightened. 'Oh, I bet my frigging car seat is covered in the stuff'

She thrust the torch into James Corbett's free hand.

'Frigging coppers,' she said and rushed out of the barn.

Angel was glad to see her go.

Corbett rubbed his chin.

Moss finished off fastening Angel's wrists then looked at James Corbett for his approval.

Angel felt several hard tugs at his wrists. The tie was very tight. Very tight indeed.

'That should do it, Mossy, yes.'

The two men left. The barn door was closed with a bang and Angel was left in darkness.

It was a relief at first. He felt sick. He wanted to throw up, but he couldn't.

He had to escape that very tight fastening of his wrists. It was fortunate that he had that apple between his hands. Because of that, he expected to escape from the rope in a few seconds.

Angel had employed an old escapology trick perfected by the great Harry Houdini, who used a tennis ball painted flesh colour to match the colour of his skin. He palmed it, easy for him, and then as the rope was being looped round his wrists, he worked the ball into a position between his wrists so that it felt tight to the person tying him up — indeed it was tight, very tight — but the person tying him up didn't realize that a ball was between the wrists he was tying together. The fastening could be checked and it would seem very secure. Indeed it was secure. Subsequently, at the right moment, though, it was a simple matter to squeeze the ball down to the fingers and let it drop to the floor and thereby have enough room in the rope to wriggle free. That's just what Angel did. But he didn't have a ball. He had used an apple.

The apple dropped on to the barn floor. The rope loosened and he stuffed it in his pocket. He could now see light showing underneath and down the sides of the barn doors. It was coming daylight. He crossed to the doors to see if they were locked and, as he expected, they were. He would be able to read his watch dial if he put his wrist to the gap. It was 5.30 a.m.

He frowned and rubbed his chin as he wondered what had happened to Ron Gawber and Waldo White and his armed team. They clearly had not followed him there. Ron Gawber couldn't have known what had happened because he was out of contact, but Waldo would have worked out from the interrupted commentary on the phone that he had run into trouble. However, he clearly had missed making contact with Laura's car, and was therefore unable to follow it to the farm. It was then that Angel realized that nobody knew where he was. He was on his own. He was wounded, unarmed and without a phone or transport. It was four on to one and they had at least one firearm each.

He had known better days.

CHAPTER THIRTEEN

As the light improved he searched round the barn. He kicked the thin covering of straw about but found nothing interesting underneath; it was just a dry, hard, earth floor. On the wall near the door were four large pegs holding an assortment of riding tack, and long and short ropes for leading and training horses or ponies. Looking upwards were crossbeams that formed the simple roof structure. There were no windows or other doors. That was about it.

He spent some time meandering round the barn, listening for the sound of footsteps on the gravel. He returned to the tack and ropes hanging from the pegs on the wall and spent a little time taking stock of what there was. Then he coiled up three long lengths of rope and threw them separately over a crossbeam at the back of the barn while still holding the ends. He made a noose at those ends of the ropes, then kicked some straw over them to conceal them. He then looked round the barn again, rubbed his chin and ran his hand through his hair. He dug into his pocket and pulled out the rope that had so recently held his wrists together so securely. He unravelled it, tied a simple knot in it about twelve inches from the end, then draped it round his neck so that he would be able to grab it from there quickly when necessary.

The sun was bright now and beams of light shone through narrow slits around the doors on to the barn floor.

He dashed across to the doors to see if he could see anything useful outside. He would like to have been able to see the front door of the house, the patio area and the part of the gravel drive leading up to the barn door, but he could see none of that. As he tried various positions, he noticed a knot in a length of timber in the wall about 3/8" in diameter. It seemed likely that it was ideally positioned. It stood proud of the face of the timber, so he reached into his pocket and pulled out a little pearl-handled fruit knife he always carried. With a bit of pressure and care, he eased out the knot and a perfect spyhole was created. And only just in time. He put his eye to it and saw the front door of the house open and Moss come out. The Sten gun was hanging from his shoulder by a strap.

Angel's heart leapt. His pulse began to thump again, seeming to make more noise than a helicopter. He saw Moss walk across the gravel towards the barn door.

Angel quickly retreated to the pole nearest the door, snatched the rope from round his neck, wrapped it tightly round his right hand, put his hands behind the pole and grabbed the other end tightly by his left hand. Then he dropped his head down on to his chest and closed his eyes.

He heard the barn door open followed by a few footsteps. There was a pause.

'Come on, Angel,' Moss said. 'Wakey. Wakey.'

Angel didn't move.

He heard him come towards him.

'Come on, Angel.'

Moss came a little nearer.

'Are you all right? Wakey wakey.'

There was a pause. He came closer still.

'Do you want something to eat?'

Angel could feel his breath on his cheek. It smelled of cheap brandy. Another pause.

Then he felt Moss's hand yank his head back by his hair. 'Come on, Angel,' he said, holding on to it for a second or two, then he let it go.

With the speed of light, Angel brought both hands round from behind the pole, turned him sideways, put the rope under Moss's chin and pulled like hell.

Moss tried with one hand to remove Angel's grip, but he made no impression. The Sten dropped to the ground, making a rattle. Moss applied both hands to ease away the rope, but Angel had the purchase and the strength. He maintained the grip. Moss's face was turning white but he was still struggling. They rolled on to the ground. Angel on top. He was determined. It was his life or Moss's. Seconds passed. Moss's eyes closed. He stopped struggling. He was either dead or unconscious. Angel released his grip cautiously. He stood up, kicked the Sten gun to his place by the knot hole, then dragged Moss across the floor until he was under the horizontal roof beam. He put the noose round his feet and pulled the rope tight, then he kept pulling until the only part of Moss's body on the ground were his shoulders and the back of his head. Angel then tied it off round one of the big hooks holding the tack. He straightened up. He felt a bit swimmy. He shook his head. He went back to look at Moss. Colour was returning to the man's face and he was breathing. Angel nodded with satisfaction.

He dashed over to the knot hole and took up his position. There was nothing happening out there, so he brushed the dust off his trousers and coat. Dust was sticking to the blood-covered area but there was nothing he could do. He picked up the Sten gun and familiarized himself with the parts. He unclipped the magazine, confirmed that it was loaded, checked the breech and discovered that it already had a round up it. It pleased him. He replaced the magazine, then held the gun in both hands in the firing stance. For a lightweight, close-combat weapon made in the 1950s, the balance felt absolutely right. He put the gun on the floor.

The barn door was left swinging open.

There were groans from the man partly suspended from the beam.

Angel looked through the knot hole. He saw the heavy growth of ivy on the house and was considering whether it was thick enough to press into it to conceal himself, when the house door opened and James Corbett came out. He was frowning and looking around. He must have noticed the barn door swinging loose. His eyes seemed to settle on it.

It set Angel's pulse thumping again.

Corbett stepped out on to the gravel, taking out his Walther PPK/S as he made his way noisily towards the barn. Angel picked up the Sten gun and waited behind the door. Corbett came in. 'Are you there, Mossy?' he said.

From his semi-suspended position, Moss said: 'I'm here, boss. But watch out, Angel has —'

Before Moss could say any more, Angel tapped Corbett on the temple with the Sten and the big man went down to the floor like a copper's helmet in a pub brawl.

Angel kicked the Walther away and dragged Corbett up to a position under the beam eight feet from Moss.

Moss said: 'You shouldn't have frigging done that, Angel. Lloyd'll not let you get away with this.'

Angel ignored him. He put the noose over Corbett's feet and pulled the rope tight, raising him, like Moss, high enough to leave only his shoulders and head on the floor. He tied him off and anchored the rope on the pegs where the tack had been. He picked up the Walther, stuck it in his pocket and straightened up. He didn't feel quite right in the head. He felt a bit swimmy again. He must keep going. His forehead was sticky. He wiped it with his sleeve and went over to the somnolent body of James Corbett, padded him down, reached into a pocket and took out a mobile phone. His face brightened. He switched it on and tapped in a number. Then he heard a sound outside. He cancelled the call and rushed over to the knot hole. He looked through it. There was nothing there.

He heard moans and groans. James Corbett was coming round.

'What's going on, Angel?' he called. 'What's your frigging game? Let me out of this! I can't do to be in this position. I'll throw up.'

'Shut up and keep quiet,' Angel said.

'You'll not get Lloyd as easily as you've caught me,' James Corbett said.

'I told him that,' Moss said.

'You'll pay for this, Angel, when I get out of this, I promise you.'

Angel looked across at the two men in the suspended position and said, 'Shut up, the pair of you, before I give you a hot lead enema to remember me by.'

They immediately stopped talking, but he knew he would not be able to rely on their silence if they thought that Lloyd or Laura were in the vicinity. He rubbed his chin a few moments and smiled to himself.

He glanced through the knot hole. There was nobody in sight. He looked across at the dark green ivy growing on the house. It was pretty thick.

He turned back to the two prisoners. 'I am just nipping out. Have a look round. Keep absolute silence. Just give me ten minutes and then make as much noise as you like. All right? A good ten minutes. Understand?'

There was no reply.

He picked up the Sten and made for the door. 'Ten minutes, that's all,' he said. 'Goodbye.'

He went out of the barn, left the door swinging, and ran the ten feet straight across the gravel. He couldn't avoid making a noise. He made straight for the ivy and pressed his back into it hard against the wall. It was good enough cover if nobody looked in your direction and you weren't expected to be there.

A few seconds later, he heard James Corbett and Moss begin to kick up a racket. He smiled at the predictability of the two men. 'Lloyd! Lloyd! Come here, Lloyd. In the barn, Lloyd. Come here. Quickly!'

It sounded as if they were calling a dog.

The house door eventually opened and closed quickly. Angel heard it. He pressed himself further back into the wall, licked his lips and gripped the Sten.

The chorus continued. 'Lloyd! Lloyd! Come here, Lloyd. In the barn, Lloyd. Come on. Hurry up. He's getting away.'

Angel heard running feet kicking through the gravel towards the barn. Then he saw him. Lloyd Corbett. As he reached the barn door, Angel raised the Sten and said, 'Freeze.'

Lloyd Corbett stopped running, turning to face him with eyebrows raised and eyes wide open. He slipped his right hand swiftly to his pocket.

Angel pointed the Sten at Lloyd Corbett's feet and pulled the trigger. It sprayed six or seven rounds into the gravel. The grey stuff jumped into the air four or five inches.

'Put your hands up,' Angel said.

Lloyd Corbett's eyes opened even further. He whipped his empty hand out his pocket and put both hands in the air. There was silence from Moss and James Corbett.

'I always mean what I say, Lloyd. Now you can go carefully back into that pocket, take out that gun with your fingertips and throw it down in front of you.'

'All right. All right. But don't shoot,' Lloyd Corbett said.

Angel's lips tightened back against his teeth. 'Don't worry,' he said. 'I wouldn't *wound* you, Lloyd. If you compel me to pull this trigger, you would be off this planet quicker than a judge could say "life". I never miss. I've got a mantelshelf full of silverware to prove it.'

'Yes. Yes,' he said, tossing the Beretta on to the gravel in front of him.

'Thank you. Now move slowly into the barn.'

He followed him, picked up the Beretta and put it in his pocket on the way. Bending down made him feel a bit dizzy. He shook his head to clear it. He was aware of invisible cobwebs cluttering up his thinking, and his eyelids were heavy. He must keep going.

Lloyd Corbett saw his brother and Moss tied up. He blinked. His jaw tightened. He shook his head.

They stared back at him in surprise and anger.

Using the Sten gun as a pointer, Angel directed Lloyd to the place under the beam about eight feet away from his brother.

'There,' he said. 'Now get down there. Face down, but keep your hands up.'

Lloyd Corbett gawped at him. 'It's dirty down there.'

'Hurry up,' Angel said and pointed the Sten at him, 'or do you want me to assist you?'

Lloyd Corbett dropped down on to the barn floor.

The two men already roped up watched every move in silence.

Angel found the noose he had prepared, and, with one hand, threaded it over the man's feet.

'Now turn over, Lloyd,' he said.

Angel grabbed the suspended rope and straightened up. As he did so, he felt dizzy again and shook his head.

All three men saw him.

Lloyd Corbett sniggered. 'Aren't you well, Inspector?'

James Corbett said: 'Do you need a rest, Mr Angel?'

Angel's lips tightened. He hadn't been as angry for years. His chest burned like a bucketful of red coals. He pointed the Sten gun at the wall of the barn behind them and pulled the trigger, letting off a short burst.

The three men on the floor froze.

'Well enough to pull a trigger, gentlemen,' he said. Then he grabbed the rope extravagantly, pulled Lloyd Corbett to the same height as the others and tied it off.

He checked the fastenings of the other two men then wandered away from them. That second burst of the Sten could hardly have gone unnoticed by big Laura, who must be somewhere around the place.

'Hey, Inspector Angel, sir,' James Corbett said lightly.

'What?'

'Before you…kill us…will you tell us…you must be…tell us…are you The Fixer?'

'I'm not going to kill you, not unless you try to escape. And I'm not The Fixer. You know *exactly* who I am. But I know that Charlie Drumme set The Fixer to dispose of you and your brother, and I have now worked out that it was you, Lloyd, who knocked out those four poor innocent men at The Feathers with chloroform and broke their trigger fingers, because you thought that one of them — although you didn't know which — was certain to be The Fixer. You wanted to push up the odds of you both staying alive. As it happens, you were wrong on all four counts. He wasn't at The Feathers that night. I shouldn't worry any more about him. You should be pretty safe for the next twenty years…in Belmarsh.'

Corbett didn't reply. Nobody said anything.

Angel still had to deal with big Laura. He shouldered the Sten gun, crossed the barn to the corner and peered through the knot hole. It was as quiet as 'Solitary' on a Sunday in Dartmoor.

She must be *somewhere*. After a few moments, he went out of the barn, closed the door and put the bar across. The bright sun made his eyes smart. He shielded them with a hand; he had never experienced that before. He surveyed the front of the house and the patio. He held the Sten at the ready. He didn't intend being caught out by her.

Suddenly he heard the roar of a car engine on his left. It came from the outbuilding next to the barn. The roar continued as the Mercedes leapt out and passed him. Big Laura was at the wheel. Her huge face was scarlet. Her jaw set. The car shot out of the garage on to the gravel drive. She waved a gun menacingly from the open car window as it passed him.

Angel pulled up the Sten and yelled out, 'Stop the car. Put your hands up.'

A bullet whistled past his ear. Then another over the other ear.

He dropped to the ground. The car turned left on to the drive, spraying gravel up on both sides and to the rear. From the ground, he fired a burst at it from the Sten, peppering holes in the tailgate door and rear window.

Big Laura screamed. The car stopped with a screech of brakes. The suspension rocked and squeaked.

'*My car!*' she yelled. 'Stop it, Angel. *Stop it!*'

The car door opened and closed. His ears pricked up. From the ground, he saw big feet in white sandals shuffle through in the silver gravel towards him.

'I give in, Inspector,' she said. 'Just look at my car. Don't shoot at my car anymore. I surrender.'

He leaned on the car to help get himself to his feet. 'Very well. Drop your gun and come round with your hands up.'

'I am not armed, Inspector.'

Laura had her hands in the air but with a small pistol pointing straight at his head.

When he saw it, his heart leaped and he raised the Sten. She pulled the trigger. It clicked but nothing happened. She tried again. It clicked again.

'Drop it,' he said, his heart pounding.

Her face went pale. Her lip quivered. She opened her fingers and let the small pistol fall to the ground.

He felt dizzy again. This time he couldn't see straight. He squinted at her and shook his head. '*That* was your last mistake,' he said. He shook the Sten at her and said, 'And *this* is loaded.'

She bit her lip.

'Stay there. Don't move,' he said, and holding the Sten at the ready he went round to the driver's door, opened it, searched the duster pocket in it, the glove compartment under the dashboard, found a small handbag, tossed it into the back seat, then he stepped away from the car and said, 'Get in. You are driving.'

He watched her climb into the driver's seat then closed the door. He opened the offside back door, got into the back and flopped back on to the soft, luxurious seat. He was very tired. He positioned the Sten safely on his knee, dipped into his pocket for the mobile phone he had taken from James Corbett and tapped in a number. As he heard it ring out, he said, 'Now then, Laura. You are under arrest for a list of charges longer than a police manual, so let's have a quiet, safe, uneventful drive to Bromersley nick. If I have any trouble from you, be assured, I am in a perfect position from back here to shoot off your earlobes. Both of them, *to match, if necessary.*'

CHAPTER FOURTEEN

There was a posse of police and police vehicles waiting at the front of Bromersley police station when the Mercedes driven by big Laura pulled up at the front steps.

Angel lowered the window and quickly directed Waldo White and the FSU to the farm to arrest the Corbetts and Cecil Moss; he handed big Laura over to WPC Leisha Baverstock, who took her down to the cells; he passed the three guns to Scrivens and instructed him to hand them to the duty sergeant at the secure store. Then he climbed out of the car. Gawber and Ahmed followed him down to his office when they noticed the blood on his side.

'You're wounded, sir,' Gawber said.

'You need a cup of tea, sir,' Ahmed said.

'It's nothing,' Angel said. 'You must get charge sheets organized for these four villains.'

'With lots of sugar in it,' Ahmed said. He rushed off.

'There's blood all over,' Gawber said. 'You'll have to go to hospital.'

'Yes. Yes,' Angel said impatiently. 'Are you listening to me?'

'There's blood dripping on the floor, sir. I'll send for an ambulance.'

The phone rang. Angel snatched it up. It was Helpman.

'Can you talk, Inspector?' he said mysteriously.

'Yes. Yes, of course. What is it?'

'I got that information. You said a hundred pounds.'

Angel frowned. 'I said fifty, and that was for the whereabouts of the showdown between the Corbetts and The Fixer, and the name of The Fixer.'

'Yes. Yes. Not the name of The Fixer, Inspector. My informant wouldn't go that far. And if he would have, the price would have been five hundred at least. But the other you have just said, yes.'

'All right, Mr Helpman. You are on.'

'The Corbetts are expecting to talk turf rights with Charlie Drumme, but Drumme knows nothing about it. Instead his place will be taken by The Fixer. The Fixer is on ten thousand pounds for a clean, straight kill of both Corbett brothers. Aaron Moss, Cecil Moss's double-crossing brother, has arranged a business meeting there tonight, supposedly between the Corbett brothers and Charlie Drumme, except that Charlie Drumme knows nothing at all about it. *The Fixer is going to be there instead.* Are you on for paying me a hundred or not?'

Angel rubbed his chin. 'I'll tell you what I'll do, Mr Helpman,' Angel said with a grin. 'If The Fixer kills the two Corbetts, I'll pay you a hundred. If The Fixer is caught I'll pay you fifty. Fair enough?'

'Yeah. All right, Mr Angel,' Helpman said. 'You're on.'

'Where and when?'

'It's tonight. That's why I'm phoning. It's at Robinson's Repository and Removals, Canal Road.'

'What time?'

'I dunno.'

Angel smiled, returned the phone to its cradle and turned to Gawber. 'Did you catch all that? It was a snout of mine.'

'You want the FSU to be there to arrest the Corbetts and The Fixer?'

'No,' he said firmly. 'Down there? At Robinson's Repository and Removals, Canal Road. In the dark? It would be a bloodbath. I don't want any police anywhere near there.

There'll be lead flying around and nobody will know who's firing at who in that place at night. Up those ginnels and passageways. You mustn't go anywhere near.'

Gawber frowned. 'You've got me, sir.'

'Well, listen up, Ron. Charlie Drumme has a contract out on the Corbett brothers. He wants them out of Bromersley. He's paying The Fixer to murder them both.'

Gawber still looked confused.

'If the Corbett brothers were free,' Angel said, 'and went there, they would be shot down by The Fixer like clay pipes at a fairground. But they won't be, will they? They'll be up here, locked up, safe and sound.'

Gawber nodded.

'Doesn't seem justice, does it?'

Gawber said, 'And did you say Charlie Drumme knows nothing about it, sir?'

Angel said, rubbing his chin. 'I did. I did.'

'But we don't know where he is, sir. We can't contact him.'

There was a knock on the door.

It was Ahmed. 'The ambulance is here, sir.'

Angel said: 'He was in hospital, last I heard.'

Two ambulancemen rushed in.

'Come along, sir. Let's have a look at you… Oh, I see. Can you walk, sir?'

'Yes, thank you. Can't you slap a bandage on it, or something, here?'

'No. We'll soon have you in hospital, sir.'

'Hospital? Will I have to go to hospital?'

'Yes. They'll soon sort it out.'

Angel turned back to Gawber. 'I'll see to that little matter, Ron,' he called out. 'Leave it to me.'

The phone rang.

'CID, PC Ahaz. Good morning. Can I help you?'

'Yes, Ahmed. I'm on one of these damned ward phones. Can't hold on. I'll run out of ten pences. I want to speak to Ron Gawber.'

Ahmed gave a little gasp. 'Oh, yes, sir. Good morning, sir. Are you all right? Did you have a good night?'

'Yes. Yes. Of course I'm all right. I want Ron Gawber urgently.'

'He's not about, sir. He's not in here. I'll see if I can find him. There was a bit of a do down at that deserted warehouse on Canal Road. He might be down there. You might get him on his mobile. Or I could phone him and get him to phone you.'

Angel said: 'What happened? What happened?'

'Don't know, sir.'

Angel sighed. 'I want to know what happened. I haven't got Ron Gawber's number and I haven't got a mobile.'

'I could get him to phone *you*, sir. What's your number?'

'This phone doesn't accept incoming calls.'

Angel heard a click in the earpiece followed by a high-pitched whining note. His lips tightened. He slammed down the handset, swung his legs out of bed and sat on the edge, then began looking down for something to put on his feet.

A sister pushed open the door and stood in front of it. 'You've a visitor,' she said. 'It's a bit early, but seeing as though your temperature is normal, you can go home, if you take things easy. But you need to rest for seven days. And you'll need some antibiotics. Then you come back here for a dressing tomorrow. All right?'

Angel beamed. 'Yeah. Great. Where's my clothes?'

'You have to come back *tomorrow*. *Tomorrow*, do you hear me?'

'Yes,' he bawled. 'I speakee de Englaisais.'

She shook her head disapprovingly. She went out and the door slammed.

A moment later Gawber came in.

Angel looked up optimistically. 'Well, what happened?' He pointed to the chair by the bed.

'Are you all right, sir?'

'Yes,' he said impatiently. 'What happened then?'

'Somebody from Sebastopol Terrace rang in at 2.15 this morning and said they'd heard gunshots being fired from the warehouse on Canal Road. They heard about ten shots in all.'

Angel looked serious and intent. He rubbed his chin.

'DI Asquith was on duty,' Gawber said. 'He turned out the FSU. He rang me to represent Bromersley CID. We went down together to Canal Road. Got there about four o'clock. Dead quiet. We waited thirty minutes.'

'Yes. Yes. Any girls around?'

Gawber shook his head. 'I think the gunshots had frightened them off.'

'Thank God for that. Go on.'

'The men from the FSU found a dead body. Four bullets in him.'

'Well, whose was it?'

'It was Charlie Drumme.'

Angel sighed. He wrinkled his nose. He felt uncomfortable.

Gawber noticed and said, 'He had it coming to him.'

Angel rubbed his hand across his mouth. 'Did you find...anybody else?'

Gawber shook his head.

Angel's eyebrows shot up.

'There was a trail of blood. He must have been wounded. The dogs picked it up...out on to Canal Road, where he must have parked his car.'

'They might get his DNA,' he bawled.

Gawber nodded. 'A sample is on its way to Wetherby.'

'Ah!' Angel said, his eyes twinkling.

The two men were quiet for a few moments, then Gawber said, 'How did you manage to see Charlie Drumme and kid him on about the so-called meeting with the Corbetts?'

'I didn't. I had intended to, of course, but when I got here and enquired, I discovered he had been discharged yesterday morning.'

Angel and Gawber looked at each other with jaws dropped.

'Well, who told him, then?'

'It couldn't have been the Corbetts, Cecil Moss or Laura,' Gawber said. 'They were down in our cells. Nobody else knew.'

Angel's head came up. 'Except… Aaron Moss. He might have worked it out if he had been trying to contact Cecil or he had seen any activity at the farm.'

Gawber frowned. 'Aaron Moss?'

'There's nobody else,' Angel said. 'It was no secret that he didn't get on with Drumme. No point in wasting The Fixer's talent. That *must* be it,' he added with a smile. He was much relieved and nodded with satisfaction.

'Come in. Sit down. Got a doctor's note saying you wouldn't be back for another week,' Harker said, with all the charm of a prison cook emptying the slop bins into the pig-swill lorry in the quadrangle at Strangeways.

Angel nodded courteously. He suspected that the prune and cod liver oil extract with the nuts and oats and straw he had had for breakfast was still occupying a position high on his chest instead of being kneaded comfortably in his small, mean, over-acidic stomach.

'Anyway, good. Good,' he said with a sniff. He looked down at his desk and picked up some papers secured at the corner with a paper clip. 'James and Lloyd Corbett and Cecil Moss were promptly recovered by the FSU in that barn where you had left them, and those three villains together with that woman, Laura something or other, have been to court and sent on remand to Doncaster. Also, in your absence, Gawber has done a comprehensively sound job in assembling the many charges against the four of them. The CPS seems content. So the Corbett gang seems to be entirely satisfactorily dealt with and needs no more attention until the Crown Court later on this year.'

Angel nodded. "Yes, sir. I understand that.'

Harker reached forward for a pink A5-size paper with till receipts, bills, vouchers, et cetera stapled to it. He wrinkled his nose. 'Now, there's a matter of your expenses.'

Angel frowned. Harker always found something wrong with them. He licked his lips.

"There's this ten pounds. It says "ten pounds paid to woman". It doesn't give her name.'

'No. Well, I didn't know her name, sir.'

'Well, what did you give her the money for?'

'It could easily have been as much as a hundred pounds, sir.'

'A hundred pounds? What do you mean? What was it *for*?'

Angel licked his lips. 'You could say 'services rendered', I suppose.'

'What services? What does she do?'

'She's a prostitute on Canal Road, sir.'

Harker stared at him, jaw dropped, mouth open and speechless.

Angel realized what Harker had made of it. 'No, sir,' he said quickly. 'She didn't — It wasn't — It was for *tipping* me off, sir.'

His face went scarlet. '*For tipping you off*?' he bawled.

Angel sighed. 'I gave her the ten pounds to phone me on her mobile when big Laura appeared on the scene. That's all, sir. Perfectly innocent, I assure you.'

Harker put a big pen stroke through the amount. 'Can't pay for expenses without a chitty or alternatively a traditional accepted disbursement that cannot be accounted for by a chitty or receipt.'

Angel's head came up. His fists clenched. 'It was for information that led to the arrest of the Corbett gang.'

'No, lad. No, it was not. The consequence of that tip-off was a bullet wound which resulted in you claiming a new suit and shirt, four days' pay while you were off work, and the capital cost to the force of a new car to replace the two-year-old one that was torched and burnt to a cinder on The Fisherman's Rest car park on Sebastopol Terrace.'

It was Angel's turn to look amazed.

The interview was curtly terminated and Angel stormed down the corridor to his office and slammed the door. He tried to busy himself with the post, but he was so angry he couldn't concentrate. Businessmen, salesmen and even MPs were supposed to be able to fiddle their expenses, whereas he'd never even been successful in achieving full repayment for all that he had paid out. It was costing him to work!

The phone rang.

Angel glared at it, then he reached out and snatched it up. It was Harker. He began speaking before Angel could say a word.

'Just got a triple nine. A body has been brought out of Wentworth Dam wired to a pair of steps. Get out there.'

Angel's stomach bounced up to his throat then subsided to his chest. That always happened when a dead body was found in suspicious circumstances.

'Uniformed are already there,' Harker said. 'I've informed SOCO and Dr Mac.'

'Right, sir,' he said and replaced the phone. His heart was thumping. His mind was automatically running down a checklist.

He picked up the phone and tapped in a number. Ahmed answered.

'I am going to Wentworth Dam,' Angel said. 'It's possibly a murder case. Tell Ron Gawber and Trevor Crisp to join me there immediately.'

'Right, sir,' Ahmed said.

As Angel had been speaking, he had reached into a lower drawer of his desk, taken out a thin cream-coloured envelope containing rubber gloves, and stuffed it into his pocket. He stood up and made for the door.

Angel arrived at the crime scene, which was on the road bridge over Wentworth Dam, a small expanse of water two miles from Bromersley town centre. The road bridge had been closed to traffic since the floods two weeks ago, and a dirty big crane located in the middle of the bridge was dredging the area in front of the sluice gates to allow easy passage of the water and eliminate the floods. The crane driver had been loading debris and junk into a skip positioned on the road. There was the usual fleet of police vehicles including Dr Mac's car, SOCO's van and the mortuary van, with the obligatory flashing blue lights.

A PC lifted the blue and white tape for Angel. 'This your case, sir?'

'Aye. What exactly has happened? Do you know?'

'As I understand it, sir…a crane driver removing debris from the escape gates of the sluice has lifted a pair of aluminium steps with a woman's body tied to it by electrical wire. That man in the orange dayglo coat is the crane driver.'

'Thank you, Constable.' He approached the man. 'Excuse me, sir. I'm DI Angel. I'm in charge of this case. You are the crane driver? Do you mind telling me what happened?'

'It was awful,' the man said. 'I didn't know what it was at first. I thought it was a big doll or something. There's all sorts of queer people out there. How was I to know what it was — that it was a real human being? Anyway as I lifted and held it, all the slush drained off of it — I could see it had been something human, so I lowered it on the pavement. I put the brake on and went over to take a closer look.'

'You didn't touch it,' Angel said.

He pulled a distasteful face and shook his head. 'No. I pulled out my mobile and tapped out for you fellas.'

'Thanks very much,' Angel said.

Gawber appeared through the gathering. 'Is it a murder, sir?'

'Dead woman tied by electric flex to a pair of steps. What do you think?'

Gawber nodded.

As Angel made his way nearer to the white tent, he saw Dr Mac. 'What you got, Mac?'

'Nothing much. Female. Looks older than seventeen, but not sixty. Severe blow to back of head. Smashed skull.'

'How long has she been in the water?'

'There's *cutis anserina* on the hands, of course. A week or a fortnight. Something like that.'

'Thank you, Mac.'

'I'm finished here, Michael. Will you see to releasing the body from the steps?'

'I'll get SOCO to do it.' He turned to Gawber. 'Where's DS Taylor?'

Gawber looked over the small crowd of police and vehicles on the dam bridge.

'Can't see him.'

'Get me some cutters. To cut through the flex. I'll do it.'

Angel turned to Dr Mac. 'You push off, Mac, if you want. SOCO and I will have a shufti at the body and then your men can have it. Phone you later.'

'All right, Michael.'

Gawber said: 'What's cutis anserina, sir?'

'Eh? What? It's Latin. Mac showing off It's the wrinkly washerwoman effect of the skin found on feet and hands when a person or dead body has been in water too long.'

A uniformed constable came up to Angel. 'Excuse me, sir. The crane driver wants to go home. He feels sick. Is that all right?'

Angel nodded. 'Get his name and address and phone number.'

'Right, sir.'

Gawber said: 'Don Taylor's here, sir.'

'You want me? Been taking samples of the dam water for comparison, sir.'

'Have you finished going over the body?' Angel said.

'Yes, sir. There was nothing. Can't rely on the origin of any foreign hair or dust particle on the corpse.'

He nodded. 'That's right. Mac thinks she's been in the water one or two weeks.'

'And it's been running, fresh, changing water,' Taylor said.

'Aye,' Angel said, rubbing his chin.

They moved inside a tiny white tent erected over a portable ambulance table. A body wearing a heavy coat over other layers of clothes lay indecorously on top of a pair of steps, typically used by electricians, painters and decorators and workmen of all sorts. The body was fastened at the ankles, wrists, neck and waist by black plastic-covered three-core thirteen-amp electric cable.

The face skin was mostly light purple with brown patches, the hair black, straggly all over and partly over the face.

One of SOCO's team arrived with heavy scissors. Taylor said: 'Cut them at the back. Save all the knots.'

Angel stood by, watching. 'What colour are her eyes?'

Taylor moved up her eyelid with a thumb and said, 'Brown, sir.'

Angel nodded then stepped closer to the table and leaned forward. He looked at the body's hands, wrists and under the chin. Then he looked at Gawber and said, 'Look, Ron. No jewellery.'

Gawber raised his head and looked at him. 'Oh?'

Angel sighed then pointed to the corpse and said, 'It's Selina Line.'

CHAPTER FIFTEEN

Don't know if it matters now, sir.'

'What?' Angel said, looking across his desk.

'I spoke to each of the tellers who actually paid out the cash to Selina Line,' Gawber said, 'both at her bank and her building society, and in each case they confirmed that she was alone. They certainly thought it was unusual, but as she had fulfilled all the rules of proving her identity and, in the case of the building society, had applied the statutory time ahead, they were each obligated to pay out her funds in cash. They recall that there was very little social chitchat. She gave no indication as to her plans. When she had received the money, in each case, she didn't hang around.'

'Maybe he was waiting outside,' Angel said, then he sniffed. 'That gets us absolutely nowhere then, Ron. We've searched Dennis Schuster's house; we really need an excuse to search Laurence Potter's house. There might be something.'

'He seems to have kept himself clean since he came out in January 2007.'

'But he doesn't work. He's always in. And he's not on the breadline. He can afford champagne and home-visiting working girls. Neither comes cheap.'

'He has nowhere near the charm of oily Schuster, though, sir.'

'I agree, but he's another possibility. He lives nearer that phone box in Victoria Road.'

'Is that all we've got on him?'

'That's all we had on Schuster at the beginning, Ron, but I have since found a copy of *Lady and Home* magazine in his dustbin at home.'

Gawber blinked. 'His wife could have —'

'I had it checked out and it is covered in his prints and nobody else's. I know it doesn't prove anything.'

'You could ask him about it, sir.'

'He'd lie and say that his wife liked reading about country life and so on.'

'You could point out what a liar he is, sir. Be the start of breaking him down.'

'I know. I know. But Schuster, I know a bit about. And we've got him on police bail. We'd soon know if he ran off. If he murdered Selina Line, he'd not get far. But it's Potter I need to examine. I haven't quite got the measure of that man yet. And I haven't anything on him either. I haven't even a feeling about him.'

'Shall I see if I can bring him in, sir? For a casual chat with you?'

Angel rubbed his chin for a few moments. He always liked to plan his strategy. 'All right,' he said. 'But if he'll come, don't tell him what it's about. Just tell him it's a general chat. That might even kindle his curiosity.'

Gawber rushed off.

Angel picked up the phone. 'Ahmed, do you know where DS Crisp is?'

'He's here, sir. At his desk.'

Angel's eyebrows shot up. 'Tell him I want to see him in here, now.'

A minute later Crisp arrived.

'I've been looking out for you, sir,' he began.

Angel's jaw tightened. 'You didn't have to look very far.'

‘Heard you’d been shot at.’

‘It was nothing. Before all that, I set you on looking for Selina Line’s jewellery?’

‘No joy, sir. I did all the shops, auctioneers…even went round the flea market on Saturday. But I couldn’t report to you. You weren’t here.’

Angel wasn’t pleased. He ran his hand through his hair. ‘Aye,’ he said, ‘and what are you busy with now?’

‘Old lady being scammed on her doorstep by Carl Exley. Acting the part of being a solicitor, telling her she’s been left a fortune, but needs fees paying up front. You know the sort of thing.’

Angel nodded then the corners of his mouth turned down. ‘Everything going all right?’

‘Going to bring him in now.’

‘Right. Good luck. Get back to it.’

Crisp rushed out.

Exley had worked up a regular line in playing honest, respectable characters such as solicitors, vicars and policemen. People were so honest and trusting, particularly old people, that Exley was easily able to trick them out of thousands. He was remembering a constable had caught him in the market a few years ago collecting for a non-existent charity. He wished Crisp well with his case against him.

The phone rang. It was the PC on reception. ‘There’s a Mrs Henderson here, sir.’

He sighed. He hadn’t been looking forward to this. ‘Bring her down to my office.’

He had already spoken to her over the phone at The Feathers an hour or so earlier. He had told her that he thought that her sister’s body had been found. He was surprised to see her already in black: black dress, black shoes, black stockings and a black hat.

‘Come in, Mrs Henderson. Please sit down.’

‘Thank you. Thank you very much, Inspector. Thank you for your…kindness.’

Angel gently nodded his acknowledgement.

She said: 'Can I ask you something? Has my sister been formally identified?'

'No. I regret that I will have to ask you to…'

'Yes. Well, I am the only one who can, aren't I?'

He nodded.

'She…she wasn't hurt, was she? When she was…killed.'

He had no idea, but he couldn't say that. 'We don't think so,' he said.

She licked her lips. She swallowed.

'There are a few questions,' he said.

She looked up at him.

'Did your sister usually wear any jewellery?' he said. 'Rings, earrings, necklace, watch, that sort of thing?'

'On a regular day-by-day basis, she wore our mother's wedding ring on the third finger of her right hand together with a large solitaire diamond ring, and she had a cocktail watch on her left wrist. That's all. She might have worn her better stuff if we were entertaining or she was going out, but that was about it. Why?'

'There was no jewellery found on the body.'

'Oh,' she said and looked down. 'Not even a wedding ring?'

'No. I was going to ask you about that, Mrs Henderson. We have not been successful in finding where the marriage service took place or who conducted the ceremony. And believe me, we've been most thorough. Now that obviously suggests that she perhaps didn't marry the man who murdered her — in fact, she didn't marry anyone. I am sorry to keep on about this, and I know I have asked the question before, but it is vital to the investigation. Maybe the crux. Do you think your sister would, under the circumstances, behave as if she was married when she wasn't? There are millions of people who live unmarried, this way, with a partner. I mean, it isn't unusual anymore.'

'I hear what you say, Inspector. I thought I had answered that adequately before. I daresay that there might have been many pressures put on my sister, but even so, I cannot imagine that she would have settled for anything less than a proper legal wedding conducted by a proper legal official.'

Angel rubbed his chin and sighed. It was a puzzle.

'I am not saying that Selina was a saint,' she said. 'She could easily have gone wild over a man, drunk too much, been intoxicated by the occasion and been totally mesmerized by him, which might have made it possible for her to have been the victim of a mad one-night stand, as I believe it is colloquially described. However, in the sober light of day, in the subsequent course of events, I have to say that I am positive that she would never, *never*, *never* have lived with a man without being properly married to him. Believe me, Inspector, I knew my sister.'

Angel noted the strength of her answer. It didn't assist him at all. But he had to admire her. It still left him with the big puzzle of how Selina Line married and whom she married, if indeed that was the case at all.

As there was no other business to execute between them, Angel phoned Dr Mac at the mortuary and made arrangements for Mrs Henderson to formally identify the body later that afternoon. Then he accompanied her up the corridor, through the security door, past reception to the front entrance of the station and to her taxi. She had been very subdued and he was still in thoughtful mood as he saw the taxi drive away. He was turning to go back into reception when he saw two unmarked police cars pull up at the side of him. In the front one were DS Crisp, DC Scrivens and Carl Exley in handcuffs. In the second car were DS Gawber and Laurence Potter. Angel watched the cars unload and looked particularly at the two villains to refresh his memory of what they looked like. He noted that when Potter saw that it was Exley getting out of the car ahead and that he was in handcuffs, his jaw dropped. He observed that Potter obviously knew Exley and was shocked to see him arrested. Potter recovered quickly, however, and when their eyes met, Potter put his forefinger vertically across his lips, then when he saw that Angel was watching him converted the gesture to scratching a non-existing itch on his cheek. At the same time, Exley's eyes shone back at Potter's like a puppy at the vets.

He saw everything in a new light. Square pegs were fitting in square holes. Blasts of a brass band could be heard in his imagination. Bells began to ring. Ball bearings were springing up to the top of a board and bouncing down a table, hitting big numbers and causing them to light up. It was like Christmas at home, New Year in Scotland, Easter in Rome and Shrove Tuesday in Rio de Janeiro all at the same time.

Angel dashed ahead of Gawber and Potter down the corridor to his office and was at the door to welcome them.

Potter said: 'So you're Inspector Angel? I've seen you somewhere before. Can't think where. I'll have you know that I've come here of my own accord...my own free will.'

'And I'm much appreciative of it, Mr Potter. Please take a seat.'

'I've got nothing to hide.'

Angel caught Gawber's coat sleeve, pulled him out of the office and out of Potter's earshot. Angel told him something very quickly and Gawber rushed off.

Angel stepped back into the office and said: 'I appreciate you coming in to assist us with our inquiries like this, Mr Potter.'

'Well, what is it you want? I haven't all day, you know.'

'Oh. You are in employment, are you? I am holding you up? You have to be at work? I am so sorry.'

Potter's eyes travelled left and then right, then stopped in the centre. 'No.'

'I understood that you were unemployed.'

'That's right.'

'Must be difficult at this time of high inflation and rising prices to make ends meet solely on unemployment pay?'

'I manage.'

'You run a car, don't you? What make is it?'

'It's a Volvo Estate.'

'Very expensive. Is it one of the big new ones?'

'As a matter of fact, it is. So what? You didn't get me to down here to ask about my car.'

'Don't you want to help us?' Angel said. He maintained a deadpan expression.

'Yes. I said I did, didn't I? But what's my car got to do with anything?'

'Well, it has a nice big area in the back. I expect you can carry big stuff in the back of a big new Volvo Estate.'

Potter shrugged. 'It's handy for…shopping.'

'Of course. Of course. Estates are so much easier for shopping and carrying things,' Angel said. 'You do your own shopping?'

'Yes, of course,' Potter said.

Angel noticed the slightly louder, slightly sharper replies to his questions.

'It would be easier if you were married, wouldn't it?' Angel said. 'Your wife would do it.'

Potter shrugged. Then he peered at Angel. 'What are you getting at? You know I'm not married. What's it got to do with you?'

'Oh? You're *not* married? Well, of course it's absolutely nothing to do with us provided that there is nothing criminal about it.'

His eyes flashed. 'Have you gone potty? Here. I don't have to stand for this. I agreed to come here to assist with your inquiries. All you've done is ask frigging idiot questions that have nothing to do with anything. Anyway, I'm perfectly innocent. I've done nothing wrong. You can't force me to stay here…'

'Indeed I cannot, but you did agree to assist us with our inquiries, didn't you? If you've nothing to hide, what's the rush?'

He shuffled in the chair.

The phone rang. Angel snatched it up. He listened. He didn't say anything. It wasn't necessary. After about a minute, he said, 'Get a warrant. Search the place.' He replaced the phone.

He turned to Potter and said, 'About eight weeks ago, a Miss Grimond, headmistress of Striker's Lane School, reported that twenty-eight computers, a reel of black electric cable and a pair of aluminium workmen's steps were stolen from her school. DS Gawber has just described you to her over the phone and she believes that you are working at her school under the name of Haydn Parmentier, assistant school caretaker, and she is on her way here to identify you.'

'So what? When you've got a record, it's almost impossible to get work, proper work anyway. And I didn't steal the stuff.'

'So you applied in a false name with fake references.'

'In a decent society, who should have to give references for a menial job such as an assistant caretaker?'

'Those aluminium workmen's steps may be the ones used to weigh down the body of Selina Line and the black electric cable may have been used to fasten her body to the steps.'

'And the moon may be made of cream cheese.'

'Miss Grimond will be able to identify the steps and the cable if they are from her school.'

'I have been tricked. These are all tricks. I demand to see my solicitor.'

Angel's eyes flashed angrily. The camel's back had been broken.

'You *shall* see your solicitor,' he roared and leapt to his feet. His face was as hard as granite and his voice colder than the tip of Everest.

'Laurence Potter,' he said, 'also known as Haydn Parmentier, I am arresting you on suspicion of abduction, forgery and murder. You do not have to say anything but it may harm your defence if you do not mention, when questioned, something that you later rely on in court. Anything you do say may be used in evidence.'

'It's absolute rubbish,' Potter said.

Angel ignored him. 'Wrap it up, Ron. You don't need me. Get him out of my sight.'

Gawber cuffed Potter and pushed him out of the office.

Angel closed the door. He was heaving with rage. He sat down to cool off. He was so angry he could have spat nails. He ran his hand through his hair and thought about what he had to do next. There was Carl Exley to deal with in Interview Room Number 1.

There was a knock at the door.

'Come in,' he roared.

It was Ahmed. There was something unusual about him. His face was glowing.

Angel didn't notice. He barely glanced at him. He was still thinking about Potter.

'Saw you come down, sir,' Ahmed said.

He shook his head impatiently. 'What is it? I'm up to my neck.'

'You'll want to know about this, sir,' he said powerfully.

Angel looked up. Ahmed had never spoken like that before.

Ahmed said: 'At 1420 hours, PC Donohue on car patrol was called to a drunk who had crashed a car into the fencing around the bowling green inside Jubilee Park. He went there to find that the man wasn't drunk. He was dead. There was blood all over everywhere. He had what looked like a bullet wound in his shoulder and another in his arm.'

Angel stood up, his mouth open like a goldfish. It was the survivor of the gun fight. It was The Fixer.

'Did he find out the identity of the dead man?'

'Yes, sir. It was Dennis Schuster.'

CHAPTER SIXTEEN

It was almost 3.15 a.m.

Miss Grimond had confirmed that Laurence Potter was the employee she had known as Haydn Parmentier and was on her way to SOCO's store to look at the steps and the black electric wire fastenings that had secured Selina Line's body to it.

Laurence Potter had been processed and was locked in a cell with his solicitor.

In Interview Room Number 1, seated at the table were Carl Exley, his solicitor, Mr Bloomfield, DS Gawber and DI Angel. The spools in the recording machine were rotating.

'You see, Mr Exley,' Angel said, 'how you can so easily become an accessory to murder.'

Exley's eyes glowed. 'I admit to posing as a minister and going through a fake marriage ceremony with Larry Potter and a woman called Selina Line, but that's all. I swear it.'

Angel produced the photograph of Selina Line. 'Was that the woman?'

'Yes.'

'Let the tape show that I have shown Carl Exley the photograph marked Al.' Angel turned back to the man. 'Do you deny providing a fake wedding certificate to Selina Line, making fake references both for yourself and for Laurence Potter?'

'No. I don't deny that, but that's all.'

'What was your cut out of the various moneys that came showering down on Potter after he went through this fake marriage with Selina Line?'

'He said he was just going to shake her down then dump her. That's all. I swear it. If Larry Potter says any different, he's liar. I got paid £1,000 for setting up the room in the town hall that Saturday afternoon and pretending to perform a marriage service.'

'How did you manage to do that?'

'I work as a clerk there, you see, or I did. On Saturdays there's only a skeleton cleaning staff there. It just needed a card saying "Temporary Wedding Room", a bunch of chrysanthemums, loan of a prayer book and a marriage certificate off the internet. And he paid me £200 months before that for the fake references to get the job. My wife will tell you. She was there acting as my clerk. We didn't know he intended murdering her, honest. I met him on the train. It was his plan. He was coming home from Dartmoor and I was just out of Stafford. I had no idea that Larry intended topping her. If I had thought that, I wouldn't have had anything to do with it. You can ask my missus.'

'Did you always call him Larry?'

'Yes. Everybody called him Larry.'

Angel smiled. He nudged Gawber and whispered, 'Larry might have sounded like Harry when said in a hurry over the phone.'

Gawber nodded then shook his head at the simplicity of it all.

There was a gentle knock at the door. It was a bad time to be interrupted.

The muscles on Angel's face screwed tight. He swept away from the table and opened the door an inch. It was Ahmed with a folded sheet of paper. He passed it through the gap. Angel took it, closed the door, opened it, read it, licked his lips appreciatively, handed it to Gawber and whispered, 'We've got him.'

Gawber read it silently. It said:

From DS Taylor to DI Angel.

Found under floorboard in bedroom at 4 Creesforth Road, one pair Garnet earrings, emerald and diamond necklace, eight-carat solitaire ring, wedding ring, cocktail watch and June issue of Lady and Home.

Saturday 6 September was a pleasant, sunny day and was the first day Angel had been able to get away from the office since he had solved the tragic mystery of the missing Selina Line.

Angel's wife Mary had conveniently wanted to go to Meadowhall that day; she had trotted out some excuse about needing a new winter coat so he had happily dropped her off at the rail station, which would take her directly there very speedily. He had immediately headed north, up the M1 through Leeds and Harrogate, and was on the right road to the Convent of St Peter at Lower Bennington.

He was taking the opportunity that day to find the Mother Superior and try to recover the ruby for Princess Yasmin as he had promised Sir Max Monro.

There it was, the sign, black on white, which read 'Lower Bennington'. He slowed the car as he soon approached several houses, a post office and a pond with white rails abutting the road. On the pond was a family of ducklings sailing behind their mother. Opposite the pond, at a crossroads, was a church. On the side of the church wall was a small sign that read 'To Convent of St Peter'. He turned left there and noticed high above the six-feet-high stone wall, tiled roofs of several other large stone buildings behind. On the road side of the wall was a monk in a brown habit and wearing a leather apron. Next to him was a wheelbarrow and at his feet a bucket. He was holding a bricklayer's trowel and appeared to be pointing up the wall.

Angel stopped the car and called through the window. 'Excuse me.'

The monk looked round. 'Good afternoon.'

'Good afternoon. Could you tell me where I might find the Mother Superior?'

The monk stabbed his trowel in the cement in the wheel-barrow and said, 'But of course. Turn right round the back of this wall. You'll find some open gates, drive straight in, park in the square next to the bicycle shelter. Mother Superior's office is facing you. There is a sign on the door. If she isn't in, ring the bell on the wall.'

Angel thanked him and followed the directions. He easily found the office in the deserted stone courtyard and he could see through the glazed door that the small, tidy room was unoccupied. He stepped back and looked round for the bell push. But there wasn't one. His eyes alighted on a hand-bell on the corner of the wall of the small bicycle shelter. He looked at it and frowned. It reminded him of his school days. The old monk had said 'Ring the bell on the wall' so he picked it up and rang it, only delicately. It seemed very loud in the peace of the church buildings out there in the quiet English countryside. He looked round and waited a few moments. He was about to ring it again when across the courtyard he saw a door open and a slim upright figure in black and white emerged, looking across in his direction. He put the bell back on the wall as he watched her advance towards him. As she came up to him she was smiling and he could see that she was much older than she had seemed from a distance.

'Good afternoon,' she said. 'I am Reverend Mother. Are you looking for me?'

He introduced himself, and she invited him into her office and seated him down opposite her.

'Reverend Mother, I am trying to trace the whereabouts of Princess Yasmin, daughter of the Grand Dumas of Alka Dora. She was being looked after here, for her safety, during the Second World War. Can you please tell me what happened to her?'

'That war was a very long time ago, Inspector. Many unusual activities were necessitated by that dreadful war. May I ask what your interest is at this time, sixty-three years after it ended?'

'It is really quite a personal matter, Reverend Mother. Can you please tell me what happened to her?'

'It is an unusual name but I do not think that that name will appear on our roll during 1939 to 1945. I can look, of course, but, I repeat, what is your interest in her?'

He couldn't understand why she was still so cagey after such a length of time. He thought that her careful choice of words indicated that she knew something about Yasmin. Maybe not the whole story but she knew that she had been there. Of course, the name Princess Yasmin was not likely to have appeared in that form on the regular roll. For reasons of security, they would have called her by another possibly shorter name. That would be her get-out. He looked across the table at her, the classical face, big open eyes, but her lips were closed and her mouth slightly pouted. Her heavily starched wimple made her seem as resolute as a judge. As she was holding all the aces, he seemed to have no choice.

'Her father was a very brave man,' Angel said, 'and was assisting the Eighth Army in North Africa fighting the Germans. I was with a friend of the Grand Dumas, Sir Max Monro, who died recently. He had been with her father when he had been killed by a German plane and died bravely in 1944. Sir Max gave me a message for her that he was unable to deliver himself later that same year when he came here, because the Reverend Mother, at that time, denied all knowledge of the Princess. I would ask that if —'

He stopped. He saw tears in Reverend Mother's eyes. Her lips were quivering but her head remained erect. She reached down to a pocket, produced a handkerchief and wiped away the tears.

Angel licked his lips as he tried to understand what exactly was happening. She had seemed such a controlled woman and so resolute. He had obviously exposed some unhappy or unpleasant memories. He was not pleased to have distressed the lady, especially in view of her vocation. His chest burned and his stomach bubbled as he looked at her. He had always had a great respect for the church and those who dedicated their lives to it.

'Excuse me, Inspector,' she said through the tears. 'I am really sorry…to have embarrassed you.'

'That's all right, Reverend Mother. But tell me what's the matter,,,in your own time… There's no rush.'

'It's self-pity, I am ashamed to admit, Inspector.'

'No. No. No,' he said.

'It is. You see, I am Yasmin, daughter of the Grand Dumas.'

Angel's jaw dropped down. Then he smiled. At last he had found her. That was terrific. He could hear a great orchestra playing music loudly in his head.

'What was the message?'

'It was simply to give you his love and give you a priceless ruby. He said it was to provide you with a dowry. It's a stone I haven't even seen myself —'

There were more tears.

'Oh, I am so sorry, Inspector,' she said. 'When I hear any news of my father, I am always like this.'

'I am so sorry' he said.

There was a knock on the door.

They looked at the glass door. It was the old monk in the leather apron.

She waved him in.

'Sorry to bother you, Reverend Mother, but —'

'It's all right. He knows. I have told him.'

The monk looked at her in astonishment. 'You've told him about *me*?'

She turned, looked at him and said, 'No. Simply that I am Yasmin. He knows about my dear father and everything. This is Detective Inspector Angel.'

The monk stared at Angel. A smile slowly developed and spread across his lips and through his eyes. 'You knew Sir Max Monro, didn't you?'

Angel said, 'Yes, of course. Why?'

'He was my father. I am Nigel Monro.'

Angel blinked, rubbed his chin then said, 'What are you doing here?'

He looked at Reverend Mother then flopped into a chair next to him.

'I came up looking for Yasmin. It was also convenient to shelter from my creditors for a few days. Met the dear sisters. They had some problem with the roof. I repaired it. Then there was a problem with condensation in the kitchen. It was the damp course. I cured that. During the time, I was introduced to the life and I joined an order of monks. I am only a very junior novice. We have a house four miles away. I have special permission to assist the sisters with their long-awaited renovations. I walk here every day. The brothers grow strawberries. I have had a lot to learn. There is so much to do here. Looks like I might be here for a long time.'

'Did you take the ruby from your father's safe?'

'Yes, of course. I brought it here and gave it to Yasmin, just as he had asked.'

Angel smiled. 'Good.' It was a big relief. He looked at Yasmin.

'I thought it was very beautiful,' she said.

'Good.' Angel sighed. At last it had been delivered to its rightful owner. He felt as if a great weight had been taken off his shoulders.

'But I don't want it,' she said.

Angel frowned.

Yasmin then reached down into a capacious pocket of her habit and eventually pulled something out. It was an envelope. She opened it, took out the ruby and placed it on the desk in front of them.

There was a pause.

Angel stared at it. The ruby glinted and shone, sought out the light in the room and reflected its dark pink beauty out at them. It looked fantastic.

'Inspector Angel,' she said. 'What use is it to me, here, at my age? It should really go back to my country Alka Dora. There are many poor people there.'

She looked appealingly at Monro.

'And I agree with Yasmin,' he said. He looked back at her. She nodded, and he added, 'She wants you to deal with it for her.'

THE END

OTHER BOOKS BY ROGER SILVERWOOD

YORKSHIRE MURDER MYSTERIES
Book 1: THE MISSING NURSE
Book 2: THE MISSING WIFE
Book 3: THE MAN IN THE PINK SUIT
Book 4: THE MORALS OF A MURDERER
Book 5: THE AUCTION MURDERS
Book 6: THE MISSING KILLER
Book 7: THE UMBRELLA MURDERS
Book 8: THE MISSING MILLIONAIRE
Book 9: THE MISSING THIEF
Book 10: FIND THE LADY
Book 11: THE MISSING MODEL
Book 12: MURDER IN BARE FEET
Book 13: THE MISSING HUSBAND

Thank you for reading this book. If you enjoyed it please leave feedback on Amazon, and if there is anything we missed or you have a question about then please get in touch. The author and publishing team appreciate your feedback and time reading this book.

We're very grateful to eagle-eyed readers who take the time to contact us. Please send any errors you find to corrections@joffebooks.com

Printed in Poland
by Amazon Fulfillment
Poland Sp. z o.o., Wrocław

58234684R00117